Copyright ©

MW01172332

Published in The United States by S.D.Relf

Printed in the United States

Cover design by Waking Dream Artistic
Creations , Euclid, OH

All rights reserved, including the right of
reproduction in whole or in part in any form.
Without limiting the right under copyright
reserved above, no part of this publication may
be reproduced, stored in or introduced into a
retrieval system, or transmitted, in any form by
means (electronic, mechanical, photocopying,
recording, or otherwise), without the prior
written permission of the copyright owner.
This is a work of fiction. Names, characters,
places and incidents are either the product of
the author's imagination or are used
fictitiously, and any resemblance to actual
persons, living or dead, business
establishments, events, or locales, is entirely
coincidental

Just Me

Written by : S.D.Relf

Dedication

This book is a dedication to my three daughters; you are my motivation and my reason to keep on pushing through. I love you more than you will ever know, to my mom for being a powerful force in my life, to my sister's Kayla and Felicia for constantly having my back, and to my friend D.K. for inspiring me, admiring me and encouraging me to write this book, you will always be my muse.

Table Of Contents

Prologue

You never think about death until you are staring at it in the face. The overwhelming sensation of dread and regret is not something that anyone should ever experience. As I lay on the pavement on this cold winter day, I could sense death's presence surrounding me. It's dark existence was lingering in the air making every breath feel like it might be my last. Every sound I listen to plays out its dull melody. "I don't want to die", I screamed in my head. I want to get up and finish what I started. I want to embrace this beautiful life I'm living. Before all of this, I had found me, just me. Everything in my life had fallen back into a place. I got a new job, a new home, new friends, and new found happiness. Everything was perfect until now. As I lay here on the pavement, reflecting on my life. I heard loud screams, but they were not coming from me. I look to my right side and I see a man that's unfamiliar and not moving. I want to help him, to tell him it's ok, but as I try to reach out, I don't have the strength to move. My body is growing cold, and numbness creeps over me. I turn again to my left just to watch my very own blood trail down the cracks in the sidewalk as everything and every sound around me fades to black...

1. Danielle

Let me start by telling you a little about myself. My name is Danielle Renae Streeter, but my friends call me Danny. I am 31 years old, a sexy, single woman with a dark chocolate complexion with curly shoulder-length natural hair. I have been slim my whole life with hips, curves, and full breasts to force any man to stare. Some may say I got good genes, but I blame it on all the southern soul food I ate growing up. I flourished in a small 3-bedroom home in a rural town in Prattville, Alabama. Our house had a white picket fence like you would see on some old corny ass black and white movie. It was brick with white shutters and a magnificent garden in the front that my mom cherishes.

I was raised in a loving home with my two sisters, Sharon and Nicole, and my mom, Lee. My dad and my mom met when they were extremely young. They had a wonderful marriage until I was about 13. I don't know what happened, but they changed from being very loving to not being able to settle on anything. They couldn't agree on what to watch on TV, who would pay for bills, and who would drive us to school. Then it all went terribly, and they were fighting every day. Deep in my heart, I felt they got bored with each other and grew apart. My dad was heartbroken after the separation, and he decided he wished to get as far away from us as possible and moved to Chicago. Our lives became extremely difficult when he left, but my mom managed. She did everything she had to do to make sure we had the best things in life, even if it meant holding down two jobs to get it. My mom is not the one to be taken lightly. She is a strong, beautiful dark brown, petite black woman wearing a salt and pepper pixie cut, making her look much younger than her age. She still turns heads at 60 and has no desire to slow down. She was there for us, no matter what. Every event, band performances, softball games, and school plays. She was there. My mom, however, had a handful with us. We would get along one day and fight the next. Mom would joke about the three of us being so different that sometimes we didn't even act like we were relatives. She was right, and I must admit that she raised three bright girls with dissimilar personalities. Let's start with myself - ambitious, driven, and into the books. Although I had all this education, I was irresponsible with my poor choices in men, which aggravated my mom because she was all set for me to walk down the aisle one day. Next, my middle sister, Sharon, is a strong-willed woman who always makes responsible decisions in life and is pretty much a clone of our mother. Sharon never took too many risks, and it showed. I don't think she ever smoked pot or drank alcohol before because she's cautious. I suggested she needed to relax and chill, but I'm not the one to give anybody any hard advice at this point in life. Last but not least, my baby sister, Nicole, a vocal 20-year-old who prefers fun, drinking, smoking weed, and partying every weekend. She has a temper from hell and will slap your ass if you even look at her wrong. We all are profoundly different. And although we clash, we are close and love each other very much. My relocation to Atlanta will be painful for us, but I have outgrown the small town Prattville. I desire unfamiliar surroundings with new people. I have had enough of this boring Alabama scene, and I am ready for a change.

I decided to leave once I started nursing school at the University of Auburn two years ago. I finished with my bachelor's degree to become a Registered Nurse. At that time, worked at a small 50-bed hospital in Prattville. The staff at my job were so laid back and easy to get along with, and the patient load was not that bad. But I recognized that living and working in Alabama was not where I wanted to be. So I made plans to eventually leave Alabama after two years and establish a brand new life somewhere exciting.

I received my big break after passing my nursing board almost two years later. I got offered a position at one of the biggest hospitals in Atlanta -Grady Memorial Hospital. Most folks know "Grady" as one of the largest hospitals in Georgia and the public hospital for the city of Atlanta. It is the fifth-largest public hospital in the United States and one of its busiest Level I trauma centers. I would've been crazy to let an opportunity like that get away from me. The only individual who will not be blissful about my move is my soon-to-be ex-boyfriend Raynard, also known as; the dumbest motherfucker on the planet!

2. Moving Day (Danielle)

"Nicole, please bring those boxes so I can load them up !" I yelled at my slow-moving sister. I took a quick look over at Nicole, and she was standing over to the side of the moving truck, looking like she had just got a bucket of water tossed on her. Her clothes were soppy wet; sweat drenched her hair and dripped down the sides of her cheeks. Alabama heat ain't no joke! Nicole was so busy chatting on her cell phone with her "boyfriend of the week" that she moved like a snail with my things. "Damn girl, could you wait a minute!" Nicole yelled back to me. "Excuse me, Miss? " I said, irritated as hell. "I wouldn't have to scream at you if you hurry your ass up!" Unlike Nicole, my middle sister, Sharon was inside the house packing things up. She looked like she hadn't even broken a sweat and was putting the last strip of packing tape on one box. "Dang girl, I'm impressed," I said to Sharon, who had single-handedly organized and stacked everything according to size and the specific rooms around my small four-bedroom house. "I know you hate moving," Sharon said. "I hate moving just as much as I'm hating this heat," I acknowledged as I started reminiscing about when I moved in.

Although I was ready to move, I honestly loved this place. It was perfect when I moved in. The neighborhood was quiet, with many trees and not a lot of kids running around. The house was simple, set on a hill with a deck outside that I could access from my bedroom. That deck was so pretty and had been my solace throughout this crazy-ass roller coaster of a relationship I had been in for one year. I would sit out there every night and meditate about my life. I had decorated it with magnificent flowers and citronella plants so I could relax and vibe out. I would partake of the delightful aroma on the patio. The fragrance alone left anyone who sat out there feeling tranquil and at peace. Unfortunately, today will be my last night here.

It is my last day to move, and it's a typical hot summer in Alabama. The hot weather outside is scorching and humid, making every piece of clothing stick to your body. I know I will hear the complaining later from my sisters about the heat, but I don't care. Today was an exciting day for me, and I'm taking the enormous step of moving to Atlanta. Growing up in this small city terrified me of the move, but I will have to set those fears aside and take a chance. My excitement today, I admit, has me almost delirious, Or maybe it's just the heat. I want everything and every box loaded on the truck, so we can get on the road before my soon-to-be ex-boyfriend Raynard gets home from work. He is trying to keep me from leaving him, but I have put up with this dull-ass relationship long enough. There's not an abundance of tears on earth that would keep me here with this asshole.

3. Raynard for the First Time (Danielle)

March 2007

I initially met Raynard years ago in 2007, one warm Saturday afternoon at a traffic light when I was scrambling to work. I was sitting in my black Ford Taurus with the song Bartender by T-Pain blasting in my ear when this shiny gray Honda pulled up next to me. When I glanced over, I set eyes on one of the sexiest guys I've seen in a while. I tried to glance away to play it off, but the guy realized I was peering at him, and he gave me a quick smile. At first glimpse, he was gorgeous, with smooth, light brown skin, a sensual smile, and bedroom eyes. He yelled over to my car while we were waiting. "Hey, beautiful," he said with a sly grin. "Hello," I responded. "Can I get your number?" he asked. At this moment, I realized the crosswalk light had changed. "Sure!" I responded as quickly as possible before the traffic light changed. I yelled my number back at him before the light changed to green. It was pretty ghetto to yell out my number, but it was worth it. At least, I thought it was.

The next day, he called me to ask if I wanted to meet him for lunch. I previously had plans to go to the restaurant with my aunt, Katina, so I thought it would be cool to meet there if he turned out to be a crazy serial killer. Katina and I talked and caught up on the family drama when he called to let me know he was walking in. That's when I looked up and saw him. He was ... short. I am short, about 5 ft 4 in. But this guy had to be at least 5 ft, although later in our relationship, he swore he was 5ft 6 in. I'm not an expert, but how a person can be 5ft 6 in and I'm taller. I have dated short guys before, but he was really short. He had short arms and an enormous head that came with his short stature. He continued his walk up to the table when I noticed the second problem, along with his height, was a giant ass cold sore on his lip. This entire meetup was a big turnoff! I thought I had been catfished, though I didn't meet him online. We talked for a minute along with my aunt Katina, who seemed to know him. "I have known this guy since he was a kid," Katina said. "His mother was my fourth-grade teacher, " Katina added. "He used to sit in the class with her while she graded papers and wait for your cousin Sheila to walk by," Katina explained. "Sheila?" I asked. "Of all people, you liked Sheila," I said with a laugh. "Sheila has been with the same guy since elementary; there is no way she would talk to anyone else," I added. "Yes, I kind of stalked her. I will not lie," he answered. "Well, at least you are honest about it," I added. "Oh man, she was my first love,"he said, smiling. "Well, you need to get over her when you talk to me," I laughed. The three of us talked for hours. My aunt got tired and said her goodbyes to go home. We continued our conversation until everyone left. He walked me to the car and gave me a big hug. He seemed pretty nice, and his conversation was good. I actually kind of enjoyed hanging out with him. After that day, I began to overlook his height and enjoy his company.

The following week, we met up and went to the park. It was a warm day, so we walked around. We strolled and talked for hours, taking in nature's beautiful sights and sounds. After two hours, it got dark, so we then headed back to our cars. "You smoke?" he asked. "If it's cigarettes, no," I answered. "I'm not talking about those," he said. "I got a little green left over. Smoke a little with me." I looked around, coyly giggled, and told him, "In that case, fire it up." After firing up a blunt, we sat in the car for about an hour. We got wasted. But we laughed and talked about almost everything that day, from growing up in the same town to our goals and ambitions. In those moments, our connection seemed like pure heaven. Ha! Hell was on the way, though. Little did I know, he had no ambition other than being an ambitious ass liar!

We kept in contact over the phone for a few weeks and talked every day for hours. He seemed sweet and funny. Every day I looked forward to his calls until I let him stop by my apartment one day. He came over one Saturday afternoon, and as soon as I opened the door, he gave me a big hug. "What was that for?" I asked. "I missed you and have not seen you since the day in the park," he said, smiling. "I was looking forward to seeing you too," I announced, sounding too eager and horny. He walked over to the couch and sat down. I stepped into the kitchen to fix us some mixed drinks. "Hey Danny, do you have a computer?" he asked too enthusiastically. "Yes, I got a laptop. Let me run upstairs and get it," I replied. With no hesitation, I ran upstairs and got my laptop. I handed it to him and walked back into the kitchen.

I didn't bother to ask why he needed it because I assumed he was using it to look up something important. "What kind of drink do you like?" I asked. "Whatever's good," he answered. "Ok, bartender extraordinaire coming right up," I said from the back of the kitchen. I finished our drinks and walked back over to the couch. What I saw on my computer was shocking. He was watching a video with two guys fucking one lady. The bigger guy was pounding the hell out of the woman while they muffled her screams with the other guy's giant penis in her mouth. Raynard was so into the video that he didn't realize I was standing next to him in shock. I can't believe he asked to use my laptop to entertain himself with porn! What the hell? I'm not a saint by a long shot, I like porn too, but I felt weird watching it with someone I just met.

That turned me off. After drinking our drinks, I grabbed my computer from him and made up an excuse for him to leave. From that point on, I stopped answering his calls and told him I wasn't feeling him anymore. So we lost touch, and I didn't hear from him again until five years later.

4. Raynard Again? 2012 (Danielle)

It was a typical hot day in Alabama, and I was at the mall looking for a fresh pair of running shoes. The mall in my city was small, but it had a variety of shoe stores to choose from, and I loved sneakers. I had created this sneaker addiction after running at least 4 times a week to stay in shape and relieve the stress from work. The anxiety I was having from my job is a serious understatement. We've had a lot of trauma patients showing up in the past few weeks, and the ER was hectic for a rural area. The patients were often treated at our facility and then sent to a higher-level hospital because we didn't have the resources to care for severe issues. The patients who came in for concerns other than trauma mainly were substance abusers, and we had many of them. They would go to the ER complaining of back pain just to get a shot of morphine or Percocet prescription. These were the worst patients to deal with because everything that came out of their mouths was a lie to get drugs. I felt like the doctors overlooked patients truly in pain to get caught up with all the fakers that come in the ER, not in pain at all. I needed these new work shoes to help me handle the stress of being a brand new nurse. I needed these shoes like a fat kid wanting a piece of red velvet cake. As I was shopping, I thought I saw a familiar face walking by, and as I came closer, I realized it was Raynard. He looked like a million bucks today, a complete contrast to five years ago. "Hey girl, long time no see," he said." I would say the same thing," I laughed and slightly rolled my eyes. He immediately addressed the elephant in the room.

"So, how have you been since you ghosted me?" he asked. "I have been working a lot," I said, totally ignoring the ghosting comment. "What are you doing right now?" he asked. "Well, I'm shoe shopping for the perfect sneaker," I said. "Well, if you want to hang out again while I'm in town, let me know," he replied. "I will call you if your number is the same," I said. "It's still the same. Hit me up," he said. I smiled and replied, "Will do."

As soon as I walked away, I thought to myself, "What in the hell are you doing, Danny?" "You know this guy is a porn addict!" Then my other side said, "Everybody deserves a second chance." I was straight arguing with myself. A lady walked by and thought I was a crazy person. I rolled my eyes at her." I might be a crazy bitch, but I'm going to call him tonight", I said to myself.

When I got home, I called him later that night. We talk for hours. He told me he was now working at a factory in Birmingham. He asked if I could come up to visit one weekend. At first,

I was somewhat hesitant, but I agreed to visit. He lived a little over 60 minutes away, which was not too close but not too far either. So I visited. He begged me to give him another chance. So I did. I enjoyed my day trips to Birmingham, seeing him, and being away from my hectic home life. He was very romantic every time I would visit. We would take strolls in Birmingham Botanical Garden, go to the movies, and dine at the tastiest restaurants. We spent a lot of time with each other, and the dates were amazing. The added plus was being in Birmingham -the Magic City- enjoying the cultural vastness and artistic environment you would never see in a small town like Prattville. Every moment was a big wow, and I enjoyed every minute.

"Hey sweetheart, I got something really special planned for us next weekend," he said. "I can't wait," I added, feigning excitement. I enjoyed Raynard, but I was still cautious about him, especially since I believe "Something real special" is code for "I want some sex." However, as much as I didn't want to admit it, I was a little horny. It had been a minute since I explored my sexual desires. So I packed my bags and drove back up 65 North the following weekend for his "little" surprise.

I was right. It was about sex or, more so, making love. We had reached the day to take our relationship to the next level, and I didn't know what to expect. Raynard had his room all decked out with candles and light music. He walked me into the room and slowly pulled my clothes off, layer by layer. He kissed me passionately down my neck to my breast, belly, and inner thigh and back up to my lips. I was a little disappointed because I hoped the kisses would land on my clit, but he left me hanging in that department. I didn't focus on that, though. My thoughts drifted to the swelling I imagined between his legs. I thought to myself, "This dick has to be on point!" I was so excited that I started trembling. I leaned my head back, soft curls falling from my face to reveal my lustful sweat and anticipation of being entered and taken. I braced myself for him, for all of him. An "Oh my God" was on my lips, waiting to be yelled out upon contact. And just as he entered me, I ... got disappointed. He was short, and so was his manhood. DAMN! I was so turned off. I had to fake an orgasm to make him think his stroke game was decent. However, this sex was far from decent. It was appalling. I was so disgusted it was the most mediocre sex I've ever had. The worst sex you could have is with someone you like, and I honestly liked this guy. Against my better judgment, I ignored our first sexual experience and continued to see him because he was so romantic and nice. "Maybe sex would improve over time", I told myself. I prayed for the sex to get better. It didn't. But we continued to see each other, enjoying other aspects of our relationship. We both traveled back and forth from my place to his place. Then, I started noticing something. When he started coming to my new home, I noticed that his clothes appeared in my laundry. I found a whole drawer in my dresser filled with his clothes.

I'm like, "What the hell?" I called my sister Sharon for her insight. "Sharon, how come this dude has clothes in my bottom drawer?" I asked. Sharon laughed hysterically and immediately said, "Oh, that negro is trying to move in." I didn't think that shit was funny at all. "I like him, but not that damn much for him to move in!" I explained. "Plus, he has a mediocre dick, and I'm still fucking with the guy down the street. I can't have a full-time mediocre dick. OMG, what am I going to do?" Sharon, shocked, asked, " Oh, you are still letting that cheater down the street hit it?" "Hell yes!" I screamed. We both laughed. The dude down the street, Tony, is a tall, dark-skinned chiseled brother with long dreadlocks that smell like sandalwood and vanilla. My God! Tony has dick for days and knows how to work it and hit every point imaginable. Tony, however, has a woman that sometimes lives with him, so that makes him only good for only one thing, SEX! Some days I like to tease him. I would call him and moan on the phone to get him hot and then hang up. This would drive him crazy, and the sex that day would be off the charts. He was my relief from a short dick nightmare.

Raynard became an extreme headache in every sense of the word. I allowed him to move in with the agreement of helping with half the bills- the worst decision I ever made. First, I found out he lied about how much money he was bringing in. I brought home at least $1,400 a week, which was a lot for a new nurse in Alabama. He brought home $500 bi-weekly, much less than he initially said. He also paid lots of money for child support. Guess what? I didn't even know he had a child. I found a child support receipt in his work pants while doing laundry. What the fuck! I then found out that his car in the shop wasn't his car. I loaned him my car, thinking he was getting his car fixed. This was all a LIE! He started driving my Mustang to work and pretending it was his car. Every week he would get his hair cut and hang out with his friends while leaving me alone at home. I ended up paying most of the bills because he wasn't helping. He was broke! I didn't have the money flow to get my hair done anymore or treat myself to anything every week like he was. I would ask him, "Why can't I go with you and your cousins to these clubs?" His response was the same. "These hole-in-the-wall clubs are not the place for a respectable nurse," he said. But if these clubs were not good enough for me to go to as a nurse, why was HE going? So he went clubbing every weekend, staying out later and later each time. The first time he came in at 4:00 a.m., I damn near beat him to death! "Never disrespect my house again!" I screamed. He promised he wouldn't do it again and cried when I threatened to kick him out. He even made me look like the bad guy to my aunt Katina. "Don't kick him out, Danielle. He's trying", my aunt pleaded. "Auntie, he is not trying. He is a bum ass Negro," I screamed. "And I want his ass out as soon as possible."

Weeks passed, then months. After two years, I was still in the same situation with this short, bad dick, broke-ass man. I thought I was losing touch with reality. I couldn't understand why I didn't have the courage to throw this dude out. I kept falling for his crying every time. Then I started crying almost every day. I was headed home from work one day, and I thought of running off the road and taking my own life. I fell into a deep depression. Every day that I knew I had to go home to face him made me miserable inside my home. I was broke and exhausted all the time. My bills were piling up, and I realized I was about to lose everything I worked for, dealing with this lowlife.

At my lowest, something woke up inside me. "Wait a damn minute," I said to myself. "I forgot who I am. I am a bad bitch!" "So why am I dealing with this fuckboy?" "Why am I allowing myself to deal with this bullshit?" I couldn't let this go on, so I came up with a plan. What did I want to do more than anything in this world? Move away from Prattville. I had this plan from the day I started nursing school, and I let myself get stuck in a routine with a man who was no good for me or my future. I started looking for jobs that offered bonuses to save enough cash to move away from Prattville and far away from this leech of a man.

5. My New Home (Danielle)

Today is a moving day, and we have got everything out of the house. It took my sisters and me all day, but we did the impossible. I walked up to the truck with the last box when I noticed Raynard creeping up to the house in my car. "Hey, baby, I didn't think you were moving today," He said. "The big question is, how did you even know I was moving? I never told you," I questioned. "Well, I went through your bag to borrow one of your checkbooks and read your acceptance letter to your new fancy hospital," he explained. "That was none of your business, and who told you to go through my stuff!" I yelled. "Nobody. I knew you were trying to leave, so I got some cash together to get ready for our move," he said. "Our move?"I asked angrily.

I felt anger and misery from two years of settling and sacrificing for a jackass who couldn't suck or fuck, and was a grimy loser and user. I couldn't contain my emotions any longer. "You are insane if you think you are going anywhere with me!" I explained. "Let me repeat my words for your dumb ass to understand. YOU are not going anywhere with me. You stole from me. You are staying your broke ass here!"

I was in full protection mode. I had a vision now and wouldn't let Raynard or anyone else deter me. "Give me back MY keys to MY Mustang! Get your shit and be on your way!" I yelled at him. Raynard bucked and said, "I'm not giving you anything, and I want to go too! I can't believe you are breaking up with me." His punk ass started crying like a baby. "Is he crying?" my sister Sharon asked. "I think it's kind of sweet," Nicole added. I didn't care what nobody said. I was on 100!

"Either he gives me my keys, or I will bust him with one of these bricks from the driveway!" I screamed. "I work too hard to keep letting you take my fucking car and just use me," I yelled. "I want my damn keys right fucking now!" I was so angry I was shaking. I didn't care if he was crying, begging, or pleading! I just didn't give a fuck anymore. I just wanted my car keys back. He then walked to the car, got his things out, and returned to me. "Here you go, Danny," he said, dropping the keys in my shaking hand. "I can't believe that you are ending it like this, he added." I didn't even respond. I promptly dragged the rest of his things from the house to the curb and jumped into the moving truck, now packed and ready to go. I am done, and I am out!

Next stop, ATL.

"If it ain't about the money

Don't be blowin' me up, nigga I ain't gettin' up

If it ain't about the money

Ain't no use in you ringing' my line, stop wasting' my time" (T.I.2014)

As I drove under the tunnel on 285 with T. I. blasting on the radio, I looked at the big picture. The buildings and the lights are so fascinating to me; it's like I'm in a strange world where everything is possible, and the sky's the limit. I arrived in Atlanta at about 8 pm, and I was delighted to move into my new crib finally. Raynard was blowing up my phone the whole ride, asking me how he would go to work tomorrow. I was like, "Not my damn problem!" He had some nerve calling me; I was done with his ass. He needed to get another chic desperate enough for a little dick. This girl was done with the tears, disappointing intimacy, and manipulations. I was ready for everything Atlanta offered.

My apartment was a beautiful loft in the downtown area, with a balcony that faced the city. I was in love with the entire scene; I was right downtown, so I could easily go to different clubs, bars, eateries, and art galleries. I was very close to the area called Edgewood.

My sisters and I hung out there a year ago with our cousin in Decatur. We turned up for Sharon's birthday! Edgewood Ave. was always on point with several clubs to check out. There are so many things to do in Atlanta. I love the day parties, the nightlife, concerts, free festivals, art shows, and restaurants. They have the Georgia Aquarium, The civil rights tour on Sweet Auburn Avenue, where you can visit the last residence of Dr. Martin Luther King Jr, and don't forget Atlanta is the mecca of black culture. For a place with so much to offer this move to was the best decision I ever made.

6. One Sexy Night (Danielle)

My sisters would visit a lot for the first few months, and they were just excited as I was to hit the town. My sister Sharon was beyond beautiful. She was light brown with curly sandy-colored hair that touched her shoulders; she was taller than me, with curves to match her stature. Everywhere she walked, she turned heads. I constantly felt that she belonged on a magazine cover instead of the boring office job she loathed. My baby sister Nicole looked a lot like Sharon; however, she had full lips and a lot more ass than Sharon and me. She had the body most women paid for, and she knew it. "Girl, I can't wait to get these streets, sis," Nicole said. "Me too, and got to find a new victim," I said. Sharon, laughing, knowing all the craziness I had just endured, she responded "Victim? Is that what we are calling them now, Danny?" I thought about it. "Yes, victim," I responded with more certainty. "I absolutely don't want to get into anything serious after that last loser. I prefer a friend with benefits." Well, at least that's what I hoped. I searched my wardrobe and discovered my red "fuck me" dress, as I like to call it. It fits my curves in all the right places with leopard pumps. "I'm ready to tear this city up, baby," I said. Edgewood was on point tonight. All the various venues were packed and beyond hyped. My sisters and I hit every spot, mingling with the crowds and savoring the music. When I walked into the

24

club, I couldn't help but notice this tall, muscular light-skinned bouncer at the door. This guy kept his eyes on me all night. "Sis, that guy over there is gorgeous. I might wander over there and say hello," I said. "Girl, he's at work. Please leave him alone," Sharon yelled over all the loud music. "Fuck that, Sharon. I need to put his ass to work right now," I replied. I was horny as fuck that night, and I needed to feel powerful and sexy again.

This guy was sex in a black suit. I walked over to him and spoke. "Hey, what's good with you? I see you are working hard," I asked. "Hey sexy lady, I'm not doing much, but I see you are doing the most in that dress," he said. His accent was so fucking sexy; it was a northern, east coast twang. "Where are you from?" I asked. "Brooklyn," he said. "I actually grew up there, but I've been in the A for a while now." "Wow, a New York accent that's sexy," I said. "I always wanted to travel there," I explained. "Oh yeah. It's the shit," he said, bearing the sexiest smile you could ever imagine. "Damn," I said under my breath. "What did you say?" he asked, laughing. "Oh, nothing," I said, lying through my big smile. "Well, can I get your number?" he asked. "Yes, of course," I said, not trying to sound too eager. I took his phone and typed in my number. "Call me sometime tomorrow. I'm off work this weekend," I said. "What do you do, if you don't mind me asking," he asked? "I'm a nurse," I explained. "That's cool. Maybe you can help me with this chest pain I'm having right now, he replied with a smile". "If you would let me," I answered back. "Oh, I will anytime, anyplace," he responded while licking his lips. He looked me up and down, and I felt his stare as it graced my breast. At that moment, he pulled me close to him and kissed me. I was shocked at first, but I kissed him back. Next thing I knew, we were making out in the corner. My pussy was so wet and ready that I couldn't take it anymore. "There's a bathroom in the corner. Do you want to sneak away for a few minutes?" he asked. Although my thoughts were like, "Danielle, you don't know this man." My pussy was screaming, "Hell yes! I want you all inside me right now!" I am not the type of woman to do one-night stands, but here I am contemplating doing something bad with this sexy guy I just met.

We snuck into the bathroom, and he bent me over the sink. He pulled down my panties slowly and began to eat my pussy; he sucked on my clit like he was trying to suck the life from it. He placed his fingers inside and worked me from the inside and outside. I moaned with delight. "Oh damn, that feels so fucking good," I moaned. "Wait till you feel all of me, baby," he whispered. He pulled out his beautiful blessing, put on a condom, and began to rub the head around my pussy lips. "You want me," he whispered. "Yes, baby," I moaned.

"How bad do you want me, baby," he asked? "So bad that I am aching all over, baby," I moaned. When he pushed inside me, my body was screaming yes! He felt so good. Every inch of him had me on fire. He gave me pain and pleasure at the same time. He moved in and out of me with so much precision it drove me crazy "Oh shit, I am coming, baby," I moaned. Cum all over this dick, baby, let me feel that pussy throb", he moaned. "YES, BABY!" I yelled while trying to muffle my screams. I haven't had an orgasm like that in a long time. When I let go, I could have sworn I saw stars. "Can I call you tomorrow, beautiful? I would like to do this again", he said. "Yes, you can," I said. I felt good, but I also acted as a pure slut tonight. "This is something I have never done before. One night stands were not my thing," I explained. "Hey baby, never say never," he laughed. "I couldn't help myself. I hope I still have a job," he said. "By the way, what is your name," I asked? Eric, he said.

""What's yours?," he asked   "Danielle," I answered promptly. "My friends call me Danny,"

I added. "Danny, that's cute," he snickered. "Well, nice to have met you, Danielle," he said. "Same here, Eric," I said, smiling back and blowing him a kiss.

I walked back over to my sisters, trying not to look like someone who had just had sex in a bathroom. "Where in the hell you disappeared to?," my sisters asked simultaneously. "Oh, I had to handle something," I laughed. "Wait a minute!" Sharon screeched. "That sexy guy was missing too. What did you do, Danny?" she asked. "Nothing, just talk," I said calmly. "Yeah, I bet you were talking with your pussy," Nicole laughed. "Oh, shut up !" I yelled. Let's head back home. I am exhausted," I said.

7. The Day After (Danielle)

I was deep in thought the next day because I could not stop thinking about him. I didn't know if I should make the first move and call first or sit back and relax for him to make the first move. I was going crazy all day waiting for his call. I think I paced back and forth throughout my place probably 30 times. Everything about him, from just meeting him the other night, turned me on. His smile, his eyes, and his scent were intoxicating. I kept replaying that night with him over and over again in my mind. My body quivered from him inside me. The feeling of intense ecstasy from his mouth on my pussy. The chills down my spine as he kissed me on my neck. The very thought of seeing him again is driving me crazy. I wish he would call me so we could finish where we left off that night at the club. Hopefully, the next night will end up with wild, crazy sex.

My sisters are still up here for the weekend, so we decided to hit another spot that night. "Where do you want to go tonight?" asked Sharon. "I don't know, somewhere with a good bar and sexy men," I said. "Shit, you had a sexy ass man last night," Sharon said, laughing at me. "I know that you hooked up with him somehow because you disappeared for at least 20 minutes." "Well, let's just say we had a good time," I said. Honestly, I had more than a good time, but I would keep those details to myself. I was looking forward to seeing him again soon, but I'm just hoping he calls first. However, it was getting late, and I needed to get up, take a quick shower and run at least two laps. "I'm going to do my run, sis. You want to come?" I asked Sharon. "Alright, Miss Hangover. I didn't think you had the energy to run anywhere," Sharon said. "Girl, to keep this body, I have to make an effort," I said.

I took a shower, made myself a smoothie for breakfast, drove to my usual spot, and began my morning jog around Stone Mountain. During my run, I daydream of Eric naked, walking out of the shower with water dripping from every inch of his chiseled 6'4 frame. If I ever got to experience him wet and naked, I would possibly lick every water drop off his body. I ran almost a mile in my naughty thoughts when I got a call that interrupted my music. It was Eric. "Hey lady, I just couldn't get you off my mind, I had to call you, and hopefully, I'm not bothering you," he said. "No, you're not bothering me, but I did have to stop my run," I said. "Oh, so you like to run," Eric said. "Every day if I can't help myself," I said. "I love a woman that's in shape," he replied. I started getting tingles all over, just listening to his sultry voice over the phone. "What are y'all up to tonight," he asked? "Well, my sisters are still here, so we decided we may go out again, maybe to U-Bar," I said. "Hopefully, you are

30

not trying to find a new guy", he replied. "No, I'm saving all this for you, baby," I said in the most sultry voice I could muster. "I can't wait," he said. "I'm working tonight, but text when you're done so we can meet up later," he added. "I will do that. Talk to you soon," I said. I began my run again, and I was deep in thought about this guy. "How the hell you let this guy get in your head?" I thought. Man, all I could think about was that kiss and his hands and lips all over my body. I had to meet this guy again. My pussy depended on it.

Later that night, my sisters and I started getting dressed for the club. I found this little black number in my closet that fits tight in all the right places. "Girl, you trying to get fucked tonight," Nicole said, laughing. "I might not get fucked tonight, but close to it", I said with a smirk "Girl, you aren't nothing but a freak," Nicole said. "Hey girl, there's nothing wrong with being a freak if you freak the right person," I said. "Plus, as long as I am single, I'm going to have fun," I explained. "I just got a bad relationship with that little dick bastard, so I will have as much fun as I can," I said. "I hate you, sis, but eventually, you need to settle down," Sharon said. "I'll think about it, but settling down is far from my mind right now," I said. "I just want to show off this entire ass in this dress tonight," I said. "Well, sis, I have to admit that this dress does look good, but not as good as it would look if it were on me," Nicole said, laughing. "I got a lot more booty than you do," Nicole added. We all started laughing in unison. I don't know what I would do without my sisters. I don't even have friends, just my sisters, to enjoy myself and enjoy life.

We continued to get ready, put on our makeup and shoes, and then headed out to the nightlife of ATL. We end up hitting this club called the Ubar. This club is always lit. It has a mechanical bull in the middle of the floor called Mandingo. If you are drunk enough and want to take a chance and ride it, you might just end up on your ass. There's always some drunk female that tries to ride the bull and falls flat on their face. I'm just a little too classy for that! I cannot see myself falling off that bull in front of everybody and embarrassing myself, so I'll pass.

My sisters and I danced all night and had the most fun that we had in a long time. We ordered a couple more rounds of drinks, and by the end of the night, we were drunk as hell. Sharon was all hugged up with this one guy all night, talking and flirting shamelessly. Nicole was on the dance floor with this Jamaican guy dancing so erotic I thought I was watching porn. He was grinding behind her with his hands around her waist. He leaned in close to her and started kissing her around her neck. She slowly held her head back to partake in the sucking and biting around her neck. I could see her mouthing oh my God as she engaged in his "sexual seduction" on the dance floor. She almost looked as if his grinding was causing her to have tiny orgasms on the dance floor. I was sitting at the bar, envious of her sexual dance assault and thinking about what bad things I would get into tonight when I met up with Eric. My sisters were having the time of their life, and I was cracking up laughing at their drunken asses.

Sharon came back to the bar first. "Girl," Sharon said. "This guy damn near fucking me on the dance floor," she laughed. "Well, sister, you know that Jamaicans dance very sexually," I explained. "He wanted my number, but I'm not really sure," Sharon replied. "You are single. What's stopping you?" I asked "I don't know, sis, I haven't talked to any guy for a while. I've just been concentrating on working and that's about it," Sharon said. "Girl, you better have fun and enjoy your life, nothing is promised to you," I said. "You are so right, sis,"Sharon replied. Nicole came back to the bar, stumbling. "Girls, I just tongued the shit out of that dude," Nicole said, slurring. "I might just give him a little ass," she added. "Naw, bitch, we're going home," I said. "I don't want to go, you are ruining my fun," Nicole whined." I think we have all had enough fun for the night," Sharon said. We paid for our drinks and started to open the door. "Danielle, I don't even know if I can walk to the car," Sharon said.

"Thank God we took Uber tonight," Nicole slurred. "Well, I'm getting ready to call Uber because your asses are done for the night,"I told them both. Five minutes later, a black Toyota with an Uber sign illuminated in the window drove up, and we got in. The Uber driver took us to the apartment, and my sisters got out and stumbled up the steps to the apartment door. "I know where you are trying to go, sis," Sharon laughed. "Yes, girl, I gotta see that fine ass man again," I said. "Be safe, sis," Nicole said. "We don't want to see you in the next 48," Sharon added. "I'll be ok, don't worry about me," I explained. We said our goodbyes, and I texted Eric for his location to get me another Uber. Man, I can't wait to see him again.

8. Eric

Man, I have to hurry up before I'm seriously late for work. I've been doing this security gig for a while now, just trying to make ends meet and save up a little cash. I'm so glad I was at the right place at the right time last night because I met the most fantastic woman, Danielle. For the past few days, she's been all I could think about, and I've never had a woman do that to me. She was beautiful and intelligent, all the qualities that I love in a woman. I want to get to know her more, so I am meeting Danielle tonight after I finish at the club. She could be the one for me, but I have a serious problem: I come with a lot of baggage.

I recently split up with my wife a year ago. Well, you can say she packed up and left me. My relationship with my wife wasn't all that bad at first. She was a good girl, friendly, loving, and beautiful when we met. She always had my back, and our relationship was like dating my best friend. Things quickly changed when I said, " I do." When we got married, all of her inner demons came out. I started to think she was bipolar. Ma could really switch personalities at the drop of a dime. This kind of scared me at times. It wasn't even a month after the wedding when she started drinking heavily. When she started drinking, she became extremely jealous and violent. I usually worked at clubs on the weekend, so it's no surprise that beautiful women constantly surround me. My wife did not like it. In her eyes, I was messing with every woman in the club. I would come home sometimes, and my clothes would be cut up or on fire. She would do it so much I started hiding some of my clothes in the car.

This started our daily routine. She would drink, then we fought, and then we fucked. I began to think I may be crazy because I had dealt with the toxic cycle for so long. With all that drama and sex, a baby came. This, however, is one situation you can say out of the darkness, something beautiful came from it. My baby girl, Erica, was the love of my life. I did more for her than my wife ever did. But then, one day, I came home, and my wife was gone with my little girl. My wife got pissed with me and promptly decided to move back to Chicago and took my daughter, not before wiping out my whole bank account.

She really tried to destroy me when she left. So my main goal right now is to save up money so I can get back to my little girl. However, my marriage isn't the only situation I gotta get out of. I'm currently seeing another chick named Trina. This girl does not have a clue. Don't get me wrong, she's sweet and all, but there's no connection there. I have tried to break up with her several times, but she can't take the hint.

All I know is after I met Danielle, I got to figure out something and quickly. Just from that one night, I can't get this woman out of my mind, and I got to make sure I see her again. If this goes any further and develops into a relationship, I have to fix my women's problems ASAP. That's a problem for a later time; right now, I got to get dressed and head to this job. I pray that I get to see her again tonight.

9. Just Me and You (Danielle)

The Uber driver dropped me off near the club Eric was working. I promptly texted him to let him know I was there. He told me to wait in front of the club until he drove his car around. He rolled down the window and gave me the sexiest smile ever when he pulled up. He was driving a decked-out Silver Tahoe, with Childish Gambino Redbone playing on the speakers.

"Daylight

I wake up feeling like you won't play right

I used to know, but now that shit doesn't feel right.

It made me put away my pride

So long

You made a nigga wait for some so long.

You make it hard for a boy like that to

know wrong." (Childish Gambino 2016)

"I love this song," I said. "I'm glad you like it, ma," replied Eric with his sexy New York accent. Eric got out and Immediately opened the passenger door for me. I jumped in and glanced in his direction. He smelled so good; I was getting wet just sitting next to him. "Where are we going?" I asked. "To get something to eat and talk," Eric explained. "Ok, that's cool, but I would rather you eat me," I said. "I'd rather eat you too, baby," he whispered. He suddenly pulls over to the side of the road near a park. "You feel like doing some high school shit?" Eric asked. "Hell yes, baby," I answered. "I love a woman that's spontaneous," he said. I climbed over to the back seat. Eric started kissing me like he was starving for his last meal. "Are you ready?" he asked jokingly as He pulled his pants down. I lifted my tight dress, slid my panties to the side, and slid down on his hard beautiful manhood. "Are you ready?" I asked. I had never met someone that felt so damn good before. As I rode him in the backseat of his truck, I could feel the whole truck moving. I was sliding up and down on him in a circular motion. I was riding him so damn hard I thought he would break him. I started getting close to climaxing, and he suddenly lifted me off of him, laid me down on the seat, and started eating my pussy without delay. He paid close attention to my clit as he sucked and put his fingers deep inside me. At this point, I began to cum everywhere! I never had an orgasm like this; I exploded all over him, his car seat, and the window. "Damn baby, you're a squirter?" He asked. I told him I had never had an orgasm like this before. NEVER. "I'm glad I can be the first, and hopefully, I'll be the last," he said. "Only time will tell," I said. " We need to get to know each other." "Well, let's head to Landmark to eat and talk," he replied. "Let's tell each other everything because we have already seen each other's bodies," he added. I laughed, "We sure did and I want to do it again after we eat". "Right now, though, I am hungry. Let's get to the restaurant! " I exclaimed. We sat down at the table, and this cute waitress with a stylish short cut came up and sat at the table. She promptly asked him for our order, never once looking at me. "Damn, since when do waitresses sit down at the table and take your order?" I asked, very annoyed. "Oh, I'm sorry, my friend Eric is coming here. Are you family?" she asked. "This bitch has some nerve," I thought to myself. "No, I'm not a family member. I'm his date!" I explained. The woman suddenly got up and took our order while staring at the pad. She didn't look at either one of us anymore. "What was that all about?" I asked. "It's nothing. I think she has a crush on me," he explained. "Oh, so you are just the woman magnet," I said jokingly. "I don't try to be," Eric said shyly. "Most of the time, some of these Atlanta females just want attention, and you know how these young girls are." "Many of the guys take advantage of them and don't feel bad about it. I'm not that guy", he explained. "I bet you have guys all over since you are talking about me," he said, asking and implying. "You seem like you can get any guy you want," he said. " What made you approach the little old me?" he asked. "I don't know. You were just so damn sexy standing over there. I had to see up close; plus, I was drunk and horny after drinking all those drinks that night". I explained. "To be honest with you, I noticed you when you walked in. I was like, 'Damn, who is that fine ass woman?" he said. "It was your destiny," I said. "Now eat your food, Mr. Sexy," I ordered. Yes, ma'am," he said, laughing.

The dinner was perfect. We talked all night about everything. The conversation was great, the meal was great, and he was great. I don't know if I should pinch myself or what, but this guy seemed too good to be true. In my past experiences, if something was too good to be true most of the time, it was. We finished with our meals and asked the waitress to bring our tab. " You ready, ma? " he asked. "Yeah, I'm stuffed," I replied. "Ok, let's head out of here," he said. We walked to the car holding hands like high school sweethearts. He drove me to my apartment and walked me to the door. "Am I going to get to see you again, Danielle?" he asked? "I hope so. I really had a good time tonight," I replied. "Well, maybe we can set up another date?" he asked. "I would love that," I said. Eric walked up to me and leaned in so close I could feel the heat from his body. He kissed me with so much passion that I was almost ready for round two. "Well, I guess I'll see you again," he said.

10. Saying Goodbye for Now (Danielle)

The next day I didn't wake up till about noon. I already have three missed calls from Eric. I texted him back. "Good morning or Good afternoon," I texted. "I'm sorry I'm responding so late, but I just got up," I explained. "No problem, I figured you slept in late," he said. "We were out till about 5 in the morning." "I just couldn't wait to talk to you again," he explained. "Oh, that's so sweet. I was looking forward to talking to you again," I said. Eric fell silent for a moment. "Well, I tried to tell you mostly about myself, but there's still something that I really need to tell you before we move forward," he said. "I want to tell you in person," he said. "Oh my, that doesn't sound good," I said. "You can take it as you want it, but I am an open book, and I don't like secrets," he explained. "OK, we can set up a date tonight or tomorrow, " I said. "That sounds good, Danielle. Just let me know what day you choose," he replied. "I will, Eric. Just let me check with my sisters to see what they want to do tonight," I replied. "They are heading back to Alabama tomorrow," I explained. "How about you spend time with your sisters tonight since this is the last night they're here," he said. "We'll set up something for the next day," he said. "That sounds cool," I agreed. "I'll call you a little later after I run," I said. "Look at you! the little aerobics instructor," he laughed. "Shut up!" I responded "I like to look good, and you like looking at me." "Oh yessir, I do," Eric said before we departed.

OK, sis, what are we going to do today?" Nicole asked. "I don't know what you want to do at this point?" I asked. "What about Dave and Buster's?" Nicole responded. "What's Dave and Buster's?" Sharon asked. "It is just like Chuck E. Cheese but for grownups", I said. Nicole and Sharon liked that and were ready to go. "You didn't have to ask me twice," Nicole answered. My sisters and I went to Dave and Buster's, had a few drinks, and played games. I almost felt like we were kids again, and even though I was having fun, I still wondered what Eric had to tell me that was so secretive. I hope it's not another woman. It was just so weird that the waitress felt so comfortable sitting down at the table with us the other night like he was more than a customer to her. But, If anything was going on between them, she would have gotten pissed when I told her we were on a date. I mean, Eric is fine as hell, so I can imagine that women drool all over him. But I'm not going to be fooled by some womanizer. I don't care if it is good sex. I'm going to kick him to the curb if I find out he's a man whore. He should have been honest instead of gassing me up like this if he was truly unavailable. Let me decide if I want to be friends with benefits. Eric seems to be doing too much and needs to clarify his situation before I can go on.

My sisters and I leave Dave and Busters so that they can get ready to pack up their suitcases, to head home tomorrow. I helped them pack their bags and load them into Sharon's car. "I'm really going to miss you both so much. I had a blast this weekend with you two," I said with tears. "I am going to miss you too, Danny," Nicole said. "This week has been the best," Sharon exclaimed! Every time my sisters leave, I get emotional. I wish they could stay forever, but I know they have their own lives back home. I have to learn to be by myself for a little bit until they come back. I will have to try to meet new people and make some friends while I'm here in Atlanta. I start my new job next week, and there's no telling what it will have in store for me.

11. The Big Secret (Danielle)

I stayed up all night for a call from Eric. It was eating me up, trying to figure out what the phone call was all about. He eventually called me around 6 o'clock that evening. My cell phone rang, startling me out of my brief nap. "Hello," I answered on the second ring. "Hey Ma," he responded, sounding exhausted ."Can you meet up with me at Waffle House on Panola Road?" he asked. "Sure, what time?" I replied. "In the next hour or two," he said. "OK, I'll meet you at nine," I responded. "Sounds good, " he replied. I got up and headed to the bathroom for a quick shower. I put on some jeans, a T-shirt and my sneakers. I quickly got into my car and drove to Lithonia to meet him at the Waffle House. As I pulled up, I spotted his Tahoe up front, and I pulled up next to it. He was already inside, sitting at a booth near the window. I walked up to him, and he gave me a quick smile. "Hey, Ma, how are you this evening?" He asked. I told him I was good although anxiety and curiosity drove me up the wall. I was preparing myself for some bad news.

His demeanor was stiff, and his facial expressions made my fears grow more. "So what is it you wish to talk to me about, that's so secret?," I asked. "It's something that I should've told you from the get-go. I am married," he said. "You are what?" I yelled out, momentarily forgetting I was sitting in a Waffle House filled with people and their cell phones, ready to document any cutting up I might do. "Yes, I am married," he said. "We are separated and have been estranged for some time now. I have been saving up money to get an attorney for my divorce and make sure my daughter is taken care of," he added. "DAMN!" I shook my head in confusion and disbelief. "So why take so long to tell me, and why did you even pursue me?" I asked with a tinge of anger that could have easily blown up to an all-out World-Star event. "Just something about you that captivates me," he said. "You are smart, intelligent, and you got your shit together," he said. "I have never met a woman as interesting as you." "Thank you for the compliment, but I'm still upset about this marriage thing," I retorted. "How long have y'all been separated?" I asked. "We have been broken up for about a year, and she's dating someone else," he said. "I typically don't even think about mentioning anything about her because our relationship is definitely over!" he explained. We just haven't gotten the paperwork finished," he added. "How do I know if this is not some bullshit you're telling me just to keep fucking me," I demanded to know. "I am being absolutely straightforward with you," he declared. "My marriage with her was a huge mistake. We argued all the time, and she was extremely jealous," he continued. "I can't be in a relationship with someone who can't trust me. So her leaving was the best thing for us except her taking my daughter," he added. "Do you have a daughter?" I asked. "Yes, her name is Erica, and she is the love of my life," he said, giving me that daddy smile. "I miss her very much, but I can't be with her mom," he said. "Well, this is a lot to take in, but I appreciate your honesty," I said. "I just need some time to think about it," I said. "It kind of changes everything. I want to continue getting to know you, but my guard is up now, " I added. "That's understandable, and I wouldn't expect anything otherwise," he said. "I have really loved being with you for the past few days, and the sex is amazing, " I said. "I feel the same about you," he replied. "Well, let's finish these pancakes, and I'll follow you home," he said. "That's not necessary. I have to start my new job tomorrow, so I need to be well-rested," I said. "I understand. I will get your belly full, and you drive home safely," he replied.

We continued to enjoy our meal, but I was a little hurt deep down. A wife and a child! This I wasn't expecting—all that drama. But I do honestly like this guy. I don't know why, but something about him is so incredible I genuinely felt like I had found my soulmate. I am not the girl to fall in love quickly, but I'm falling for this guy for some bizarre reason. He's all I can think about every moment of the day. I don't know why I'm so into him this quickly? Is it the sex or the conversation? I don't know? All I know is I want him, but I don't want to share him. The only issue is that if he has a daughter, I will share him with her forever. I don't have kids, so it's a little complicated for me to understand, but I'm not the one to come in between a man and his child. I had to deal with women coming between my dad and me while growing up. That was the worst situation to go through as a child, and I would never wish that on anybody. Every time he promised me he would be there for a game or my graduation but didn't show up because of some woman, it split my heart into a million pieces. I never wish that for any child, ever. We finished up our meal and walked to the car. "I'm sorry I ruined your night," he said. "No, it's not ruined," I said, failing to hide my utter disappointment. "You told me the truth, and that's all that counts," I said. "It's up to me to decide how I will handle this, but if we move forward, you need to get a divorce ASAP," I said. "My mom and sisters would kill me if they knew I was dating a married man," I added. "Please believe me. I'm working on it," Eric replied. "I've been working on it since she left," he declared. "It's just going to take time and money, and I'm working my ass off to make sure I have the money to get this attorney to have a fair deal, he added" "I know she's not going down without a fight because she's just vindictive," he said with sadness in his voice. "I understand; my ex was hard to get rid of too, but I did what I had to do and got rid of him to move here," I said. "My life is 100% better since I got rid of him. Just do what you have to do, and I'll be supportive, and when you decide that you want to move forward with me, I will be here."I added. "Thank you for being so understanding," Eric said. "You are the perfect woman." He then gave me a hug and the softest kiss. But this time, after knowing his truth, the kiss wasn't the same.

Later that night, I called my sister Sharon to talk to her about the situation. " Hey, big sis," Sharon said excitedly. "Hey, girlie," I replied with a laugh. "How are things going," Sharon asked? "Not so good," I explained hesitantly. "What do you mean not good?" Sharon interrogated me "Last I heard, you were in this whirlwind romance and on cloud nine at the same time, " Sharon said, snickering. "Well, things have a way of changing," I said, irritated. "Eric has too many issues for me," I explained. "Everyone has issues," she said. "Choose if you want to accept it or move on", she added. "I really care about him, but I don't know if I want to deal with this drama," I explained. "Well, sis, if it is a problem for you, get out while you can. Your happiness is everything, and you shouldn't jeopardize that for some good dick," Sharon said. "You are always right, sis," I responded. " I will be thrilled when Y'all are back in town to visit me. I need a night out on the town," I added. "Me too, sis," Sharon said, laughing

12. My First Day (Danielle)

It truly upset me about the news I got. I was not expecting Eric to tell me something like that. Now, what the hell am I going to do with this information? He could be telling the truth: they may be on the brink of a divorce, but guys lie like that. I don't want to be a stupid female caught up in a lie, so I need to weigh my options here. I will not lie. I like his conversation, and I certainly enjoy being around him. At one point, I could see myself with him forever. I just don't want to get caught up, and I will not get trapped. I need to talk to my sisters further about it, but I'm terrified that my sisters may criticize me or think I'm stupid. I wish he had told me this before we even got this far in the relationship. Then he could have just been a booty call. Well, no need to think about it now. I need to get dressed to start my first day at work. I put on my makeup and pulled my hair back into a ponytail so at least I would be cute for my first day of orientation. I had my blue scrubs on my bed ironed and ready, although I thought it was pointless since our first two weeks are strictly computer training.

Grady Hospital is an enormous place, I don't know if I'll be able to live up to its expectations, but I'm going to try. I did my computer training for two weeks and was completely ready to hit the floor running. When I came in to work for the first day on the floor, a nurse named Steve greeted me. "Hey, you warmed up for your first day at work," Steve asked. "Yes, I am," I replied with a smirk. This nurse Steve was sexy as hell. He was about 5'11, with dark chocolate skin and the sexiest smile ever. He was brilliant as hell, too. "Danielle, concentrate", I thought "You are not supposed to be checking out your co-worker," I told myself. I had to admit before I got the news about Eric, I probably wouldn't have even looked at Steve in that way. But now, I have to weigh out my options. Today's work was steady. I only had three patients for the first day and took care of everything my patients needed. "I'm very impressed," Steve said. "Thank you," I replied. "Well, do you have questions before you go?" Steve asked. "No, you have been very helpful," I replied. "This was a very good first day," I said. "Well, not all days are good here. You will have some rough patches, but sometimes you have to brush it off and keep going," Steve said. "I know what you mean," I said. "Well, thanks again for everything." "Anytime," Steve replied.

I clocked out for the day and was ready to get home. I parked my car too far from the hospital and tried to walk as quickly as possible to it. As I approached my car, a homeless guy who seemed a little strung out suddenly stopped me. "Hey lady, can I have some change for something to eat?" he asked. "I'm sorry, sir, but I don't have any cash on me," I said, apologetic. "You dumb bitch, you got some money!" he yelled angrily. The homeless man got in a stance as if he was about to charge at me. "Hey man, get away from here before you become a dumb bitch!" a voice yelled from behind me. I turned around, and it was Steve. The homeless man darted across the street. "Are you ok?" Steve asked. "Yes, thank God you showed up," I said. "I was terrified! I just froze up .We don't have these homeless folks back home. That dude was crazy!" Steve looked me over, checking me to make sure I hadn't been hurt. I was startled but not injured. I appreciated Steve's concern. "Well, this is a big city, and it's a lot of homeless people everywhere you go," he said. "You just got to be on your P's and Q's," he added. He started escorting me to my car. "Where are you from again?" Steve asked. "Alabama," I answered. "Oh, I have family there," he said. "Oh, that's cool. What part?" I asked. "I have family in Huntsville, but I haven't been there to visit in a while because I work too much," he said. "Well, I could understand that. I plan on picking up as many shifts as I can when I come off of orientation," I told Steve. "Well, that's good. Maybe I get to see you more," he said, smiling. Was Steve flirting with me? Cute. But for real, I can't deal with any new interests right now. Then again, I am single. Eric and I are not official, and he has drama. I smiled and said to Steve, "That would be nice."   "Well, I will see you next shift, and maybe we could get some coffee when we get off in the morning," he said. "You got a date," I replied. I got in my car and headed home with the biggest smile. These last few weeks have been crazy!.

13. Soon As I Get Home (Danielle)

When I got home, I took a long hot bath and just thought about my day and my issues right now with Eric. My cell phone buzzed. And it was him. "Hey Eric, how are you doing," I said. "I'm doing well. How was your first day at work," he asked. "It was good. I only had three patients, and I had an excellent trainer,"I replied. "Male or female?," he asked. "He was a male nurse," I said. "Did he train you well?," Eric asked. "Yes, and he also told me I did a pretty good job, "I said. "Oh, I see. I wondered why I didn't get a text from you today, " he added sarcastically. "Well, I was pretty busy trying to learn the ropes, so I didn't have a chance," I replied. " I thought about you a lot, and I know we have issues, but I wondered if I could see you again tonight?," he asked. "Well, I'm off, so I'm all yours," I said. Of course, I quickly got dressed and put on a sundress with no panties, and I sat on my patio while I waited for him to get to the house. He texted to let me know he was outside, so I met him on the sidewalk next to his car. "I see you in a sundress tonight, and I really like it," he said. "Thank you, I said. I bet you would like the fact that I'm not wearing any panties." "Oh really!" he said. Eric then lifted me, placing me onto the hood of his car. "Let me see," he said, looking like a horny teenager. He reached under my dress and whispered, "Oh yes, she's already ready. Now let's see how spontaneous you really are." He leaned me back, threw my dress over his head and shoulders, and ate my pussy right there. On top of the car. In the open. It scared me because someone could see us, but it was so good that I didn't tell him to stop. He licked and sucked me so good, and it was so exciting that I almost forgot I was outside.

"Eric, somebody may see us," I whispered. "Who cares, let them watch," he moaned. "You like that baby. I want you to let everyone know how good this tongue is," Eric moaned. At that precise moment, I came. "Eric, Eric!," I yelled. I came so hard I thought I broke my pussy, because I couldn't stop cumming. It was like a river flowing from me. I released all my emotions, pain, and joy, everything I had inside me, all on the hood of Eric's car. If there was an explosion that night, it was my pussy in Eric's mouth. "Can we go upstairs, baby? " I begged. I was so exhausted that I could barely walk. I was lightheaded, actually seeing stars. This orgasm was so intense. Eric then picked me up and carried me to the door. I barely got the door opened when he started bending me over against the door. He grabbed my hips and started fucking me right there at the front door. I moaned because my pussy ached; I tried to cover my mouth with my hand to muffle my moans because we were close to the neighbor's door. I could see the neighbor's expression if she caught us outside. She would probably have a heart attack. He moaned as he reached his climax. "Oh, Danny," he moaned. "Wow, that was really exciting," I exclaimed. "I told you I like to be spontaneous, which means anywhere, anytime," he said. "That was very anywhere, anytime, moment," I replied. "Well, would you like to come in, finally?" I asked, laughing. "Sure, plus after this workout, I need a shower." Eric replied. "You want to join me in the shower?" he asked, "Are you going to behave in that shower?" I answered. "Now you know I will not behave," he replied, smiling. He walked me into the house as he headed to the shower. He stripped naked and looked at me, " Are you coming?" he asked. "Oh yes, baby, you know I am", I replied.

The following day I woke up to the smell of eggs and bacon cooking. I walked to the fridge and poured myself a tall glass of orange juice. I looked over at him by the stove, and he was fixing breakfast with nothing on but a towel and a smile. Oh my God, I feel like the luckiest woman in the world. But with that feeling of euphoria, there is that lingering doubt in my mind because of his estranged marriage. My phone suddenly started ringing, and it startled me. I could hear a person breathing on the other end when I picked up. "Hello, Hello," I said. The phone then hung up. This is the second time that someone called and hung up in two days. It's just weird. "I hope you don't have any stalker trying to get back with you since you have been hanging out with me," he asked, smiling. I started thinking. The only person I could consider a stalker is Raynard back in Alabama, but I think he's moved on. "I am glad he's finally gone," I told Eric. I saw a post on Facebook of Raynard and his new girl, his next victim. "Good. He can bother someone else other than me", I thought . "Oh, he was that bad," Eric asked. "The worst," I said, frowning at the mere remembrance of Raynard, but I don't like to talk about my past relationships." I told him it is not good to keep bringing up the past in a new relationship. "You are so right, " Eric agreed. "Leave the past in the past." Then, I looked at Eric and said, "Wait, you can't say that because your past is not your past, and you need to fix it." "What do you mean by that, Danny? I told you what I've been trying to do. I have no reason to lie to you," he explained. "I really want things between her and me over, and I'm making all the proper legal adjustments to make sure that is possible. All I want is what's best for my daughter. And my daughter does not need to grow up in a world where both her parents are fighting all the time. That's not healthy for any of us," he explained. I understand, but I told Eric he has to understand my perspective on all of this, especially since he sexed me up before telling me the truth.

I had looked on Eric's Facebook page. He still has his wedding pictures plastered all over the pages, as if they aren't having separated or threatening a divorce. "I can look at it two ways, Eric," I said. "You could want to get her back and maybe start over or be tired of the marriage. But for someone who is sick of their wife, why do you still have your old family photos around?"I added. "You still haven't deleted your wedding pictures or your old pictures on Facebook," I continued "If you want to keep them to reminisce, keep them; but if you are trying to start a new relationship, you might need to get those pictures off Facebook because they're sending a completely different message to me." I was hoping what I said bothered Eric. "I didn't even think about those damn pictures. They meant something to me back then, but not now," he said. "Danny, I'm not trying to start an argument with you this morning. I've told you what I wanted to do. You can either accept it or not," he said. "Either way, I'm still not going to leave this good ass pussy alone," he said, smiling. "That's what you think, buddy," I replied. My cell started ringing again. I answered. The caller hung up. "I need to find out who this damn caller is. It's getting annoying," I thought. "You better hope it's not Freddy Krueger calling," he laughed. "Shut up; you're not funny," I said.

That morning we continued to sit down and talk and enjoy breakfast together. I can't get enough of this guy. His conversations are crazy, and he's so damn sexy, but I don't want to get caught up in just the sex and not pay attention to the bigger picture. I hope he's not lying, and I hope he takes care of his business soon. I want this to be Eric and me, not me, him, and her. He heads to the bedroom to get dressed to go back home. I gave him a long goodbye kiss and a hug. "Thank you for the most spontaneous night ever. I had so much fun. I hope we can do it again soon", he said. "Me too", I replied with a grin. "That was amazing",I added. "You are amazing and beautiful", he said with the sexiest smile ever. "You're not too bad yourself," I replied, giggling. He then headed out, and I headed back to the bedroom to put on my workout clothes for my morning run.

14. New Friends

The next day it was time for me to go back to work. I am still receiving these random calls from an unknown caller that keeps hanging up. I don't know if I should ignore it or start to worry about it. The calls are beginning to become extremely annoying. I finished preparing my lunch for tonight at work. I cooked baked chicken breast with lemon pepper seasoning, asparagus, and sautéed zucchini and squash. I have been trying my best to watch what I'm eating because I know exercise is not going to work if I keep stuffing my belly, so I have to stop eating out so much. I put myself together, and I made my way to work by the grace of God. That Atlanta traffic is the worst thing ever. I walked into Grady hospital, and I was 10 minutes early. I was standing by the clock, waiting for the time to change so that I could clock in when he walked in.

Steve was looking extra delicious today in his uniform. His scrubs were creased, and his swag was definitely on point. Every female in the area stopped and stared at the chocolate God walking down the hallway. He started walking toward me with a smile that lit up the room. "Hey beautiful, how are you doing today?" Steve asked. "I'm good," I said. " Yeah, just ready to clock in and start doing my thing,he said. "That you do very well," I replied, adding a little flirt to that. "Well, thank you so much. I try my best, " Steve said. "I'm trying to get as good as you," I said. "I'm still fairly new, so I still have to learn a lot," I explained. "Well if you need me, I'm always there to teach you," Steve said. "I might take you up on our offer," I teased. I don't know what it is about Steve; maybe it's his eyes, sexy smile, or Cologne he always wears. He is like a black King. He's centered, knows what he wants, is a protector, and inspires everyone around him. I know I shouldn't be checking him out, but I can't help myself. He's everything I would want in a guy, and I wish I had met him first, beecause now, I am somewhat in a relationship with Eric, but I got a serious crush on Steve. I go to my normal floor, and I get a report for my patients. I only have four patients tonight, and all of them are very pleasant. I pass out medications and finish my charting to take a 30-minute break. I texted Steve to ask if he wanted to go on lunch break with me, and he agreed. We decided to go outside and eat our lunch and talk. Steve tells me a little about himself. He has a bachelor's degree in nursing, and he's working on his master's at South University. He wants to continue school to become a nurse practitioner. He's also in the process of writing a book. He has many goals, dreams, ambitions, and sexy to go with it. We walked back into the building after taking lunch. "I hope you don't think that this is our lunch date. We are still going to get coffee in the morning and I promise I'm going to hold you to it", he said. "Well, I can't wait," I replied. "OK," he said as he bent down and kissed me on the cheek. "I'll see you then", he replied with a smile. When I clocked out at 7 a.m., we met up at Starbucks. We continued our conversation about our lives and all we wanted to do in the future. "You know I like you," Steve said. "I liked you since the first day of orientation, he added. Wow, I didn't really know what to say. I told him I was feeling him too but that I had been seeing someone for a few months. "His name is Eric, but it's a little complicated. We aren't official," I explained. Steve seemed unbothered and actually up for a challenge. "If it's not official, you still can go on a date with me,"he said with a smile. "Well, that is true. I'm technically not locked down yet," I said. "Well, if he doesn't get on his game, he might not be able to get that at all," Steve said. "Oh really?" I asked. "Yes, really," he replied. "I do like you. I'm not playing about that", he said. "Well, when do you have a day off next time," I asked. "Maybe next Saturday," he said. " Well, what do you want to do?" I asked. "I'm just going to surprise you," he said. "All right then, I'll see you Saturday," I said. "Well, you have a nice morning, Danny," he said. "You to Steve," I replied.

As I drove home from work, my mind was racing. Am I making the right decision by going out with Steve, or am I jeopardizing my relationship with Eric? Although Eric is the bomb in bed, Steve turns me on by how he thinks. Suppose his sex game is good too? Eric might be in some trouble. I drove back to the apartment from work and ran straight to the shower. I then fixed myself some breakfast and laid down in my bed, but I had a hard time going to sleep. My thoughts were completely on Steve. As soon as my eyes started to get heavy, I got a text from Steve. "Danny, I think you are a cool person, and I would like to get to know you better," he said. "I know that you got a situation going on right now, but I want to prove to you that I might be in a better situation if you give me a chance," he added. I texted him back, "Steve will have to see how things go. I'm looking forward to seeing you soon." Steve texted back. "Go ahead and get you some sleep. Good night."

15. Steve

I am lying here thinking about Danny. I haven't liked a woman in a long time. Nurses at work come up to me, flirting and trying to go out with me, but I didn't feel them. I could have any girl I want, but I don't want to be in a relationship with somebody easy for me to get. I want a challenge. The first day I met Danny, I was in awe. I thought she was so fucking sexy and felt I got to have her, but I had to play it cool because we work together. I did not want to look like I was coming on too strong, and I definitely didn't want to have any sexual-harassment case on me. This me-too movement is the not-for-the-play-play, protecting women from some of these guys who are nothing more than predators. I tried to get close to her, but I wasn't sure it was working. Now I see after our Starbucks date. I think that she's kind of feeling me too. I know she's with a guy, but things could change. I look at it like this: if everything were all well with her and this guy, she would not be flirting with me, right? So I'm just going to play it cool and figure out things as I go. I have got to be on my game for my career. I've been working as a nurse for about six years at Grady, and I really like it, but I got this nurse practitioner certification. I want to run my own clinic and do my thing in the future. Working with other nurses is fine, but I would rather be in charge of my patients and business the way I want to take care of things. So I have been hitting these books and getting myself out of this program to have some personal time. I got the money, and hopefully, I will get this woman.

16. Trina

Eric is lying here, sleeping like an angel. He's the DEVIL. I know his ass is sneaking around, and I know he's talking to another bitch. He has been very distant lately and hasn't been coming around as much. Then he came by my house one night two weeks ago to get a little loving and, as usual, his ass went to sleep. As soon as he was knocked out. I looked through his phone and got that bitch's number. I found out the bitch's name is Danny. She is a new nurse at Grady Memorial Hospital, and I've been driving that ass crazy for two weeks. I have been calling her phone and hanging up on her face almost every day.

I know it's a little immature, but who gives a fuck? Eric's sorry ass hasn't been spending enough quality time with me lately like he used to. I assume he was going through a phase because he's trying to get a divorce from his wife, but that didn't stop him before. Last night, I got him to come after sending him a picture of me naked in the shower playing with my pussy with my shower head. The thought of me naked would make any man lose his mind, and Eric is one of them. I'm sexy, and all I have got to do is send him something freaky to his phone, and his ass is running over here. My girlfriend Sheila keeps telling me to leave him alone since he always works and we never really go anywhere, but I know this man loves me. He tells me every time he makes love to me, which says a lot. I need to find out who this hoe is and why he calls her all the time. He doesn't even call me that much, and I'm giving him a good head. Can't a bitch make him feel like I do? I'm going to have some serious words for his ass when he wakes up.

Eric woke up and looked around for his phone. "Trina, what are you doing?" Eric asked, sounding sleepy. "Oh, I just wanted to know what the fuck you were doing lately," Trina said? "Oh, man, I don't have time for this shit!" he screamed. "This was a big mistake again," Eric said. "Big mistake?" I asked angrily. "What you mean, big mistake?" "I mean, I shouldn't be messing with you anymore," Eric said. "I'm done with this whole thing we had going on here," he added. "I am moving on, Trina, so I'm out of here," Eric yelled!! Eric started putting on his clothes and trying to get out of the house. "Where the fuck you think you're going to see that, Danny bitch?" I asked. "How do you know about Danny?," he asked. "I went through your phone and read your text messages with your punk ass!," I yelled. "Man, you are trifling as hell!," he said. "You went through my phone!," he asked, sounding very upset "I bet you are the one that's been calling and hanging up for the past week?," he asked. "Oh, you know me so well, Eric," I said. "You are one crazy-ass bitch!" he yelled. " I knew I should've left your ass along, but my dumb ass came back over here again", he added. "But this is the last time you don't have to ever worry about me coming over here, ever!," he exclaimed "Stay the fuck out of my life, and don't call Danny again!," he added "Oh, when I get done, you're going to wish you never met me," I said. "You are around here playing around with my emotions, and you know I love you. You could be with me, but you want to be with bitches, all these bitches", I yelled. "I'm not the one, and you are gonna pay for breaking my heart, you sorry piece of shit!" I yelled at the top of my lungs. "Girl, I never loved you, just your pussy. That's a big difference; there's a lot more pussy out here," Eric said. "Bye crazy ass girl, I'm out!" he yelled as he stormed out of the door and slammed it shut. Little did he know I got pictures of his ass over here to sleep, so his new relationship is over!

17. Danielle

I'm sitting here reading my book on Kindle by Michelle Obama. It's probably one of the best books I've read in a long time. There's nothing like having a relaxing afternoon with a good book. I get up to fix myself another glass of red wine, and I walk back to my couch to sit back down. My phone started ringing. "Bitch!" the caller screamed on the other end and then hung up. Ok, this is getting out of hand. At least now I know it's a female that's harassing me, but why? Eric is the only explanation. His wife is in another state, so how could she have gotten my number? So many questions, and Eric is going to talk. I am not the type of woman who likes to be in a messy relationship, and if Eric has more secrets, this is an enormous problem. I think I might give him a quick call today. I picked up my cell, and I started dialing his number." Hey, baby," he said on the other end. "Hey Eric, I got a few questions," I said. "I have been getting these random calls lately, and they are seriously getting out of hand," I added. "This time, the caller called me a bitch," I said. "So now I know that it's a female. Do you have anything to do with this?" I asked. "Nope," he said. "Why don't I believe you, Eric," I asked? "Seriously, baby, I do not know who is calling you," he replied "Well, it's really bothering me," I said. "I know, baby, and I hate to see you so upset," he said. "I know you are shook up about this person stalking you, but I have a question," Eric asked? "What is it, Eric?" I asked? "Can I come to see you tonight?" he asked. "I miss you," he added. "I guess so, but I'm still pissed off about all this," I replied. "Well, if you let me come over, I can make it better," he said in a sexy tone. "Plus, I could bring a few things and cook you some dinner if you like," he added. "Oh, you are trying to get me in a good mood. That will be nice," I said with a smile. "Well, I'll see you around seven. Goodbye, sexy,"he said. "OK, Eric, I will see you soon," I replied. I rushed to the bathroom and hopped in the shower to prepare for Eric's arrival. I put on something sexy and pulled my hair up. I had to tidy up my house a little because I've been at work all week and have done nothing. As quickly as possible, I got the house smelling good and looking sexy. At about seven, Eric came over to the house looking good and smelling delicious. "Hey sweetheart, how are you doing tonight," he asked. "I'm doing well now since I am laying eyes on you," I replied. "Well, let me start cooking up this amazing meal for you tonight, then I'm giving you a massage later, and after that, I'm giving you all of me," he said. "That sounds amazing. I am looking forward to all of you," I laughed. "Well, you won't have to wait too long, but I want to give you a full belly first, so let's try to get that out of the way," he laughed. Eric cooked an amazing meal with beef tips, asparagus drizzled with lemon juice, and my favorite yams. After eating, we sit down on the couch to watch a movie. "I guess this is what you might call Netflix and chill, right?" he laughed. "Yeah, that's what they call it, but you know Netflix and chill mean other things," I said. "I thought you never asked," he laughed.

After a crazy night of lovemaking, we both were exhausted. We lay there in the bed, holding each other and talking. "I'm terrified about this person," I said. "Baby, there's nothing for you to fear. This woman is a coward,' he replied. "She has to be scared if she keeps calling you and hanging up," he said "I hope so, but I don't have a good feeling about the whole thing," I replied. As we continued lying there and enjoying each other, we suddenly heard three loud sounds. Boom! Boom! BOOM!

"What the hell was that," I asked? "I don't know, but it sounds like it was coming from outside near the street," he replied concernedly. "Oh my God, I hope no one ran into my car. I parked myself on the street!" I exclaimed. "Do you see it?" I asked "I can't see it from here, Danny," he said. "I will put on some clothes and go out there to check it out," he replied. "Well, I'm going to check too," I said, sounding like a hero's sidekick. As we got dressed and headed out the door and down the steps, I stopped. I was in disbelief. They knocked all the windows in my car out except for the rear window. It shattered glass all on the pavement. I couldn't believe someone could do this to me, but I already knew who did it with all the calls every day. "This bitch is psycho, and now she's busting the windows out of my car! " I yelled. "I can't afford to get all those windows fixed. I'm just starting this job, and I'm trying to play catch up on my bills, Eric damn!" I yelled. "Don't worry about it, baby. If you got full coverage insurance, it'd cover this," Eric added. "I hope you are right, but I don't need my insurance rates to go up because of a crazy bitch," I said. "I promise you, babe, we'll find out who it is," he added. "I hope so," I said as I laid my head on his chest and cried.

18. Trina

Oh, my fucking God, I enjoyed busting that bitch's windows out last night. Little did Eric know I followed him when he left his house so that I could see where this bitch lived. I sat outside all night thinking about what my next move would be. I would not leave here until he came out so that I could confront him, but he never came out. He spent the night at this bitch's house, and it looks like he carried up groceries, so I'm pretty sure he cooked for this bitch. He did none of that shit for me. The more I sat in the car and waited and waited, the angrier I became. By the night's end, I was so furious I started seeing red. So I got out of my car, went into my car's trunk, and got my crowbar. I walked over to her car with my hooded sweatshirt on so no one would recognize me and knocked every damn window out of her car. This is what you deserve, bitch, for messing with my man.

I drove home after I had destroyed her car. I ran some water in the tub and lit my scented candles. As I sat here, letting the warm water and suds run over my body, I cut on my music and listened to the sounds of Shirley Murdock. "Go on without you."

"Before you left me, I had it all

You were with me, and that was enough

He came along, and I forgot all about you

I was a fool, but I'm wiser now

Because you left, my world came to an end

Then you came back again. Now I know

There is no way that I can go on without you."(Murdock, Shirley1985)

This song is so depressing. Tears started flowing as I sat here, wondering what makes Danny better than me. I have a nice body. I'm beautiful. I try to keep my hair laid and my nails on point. What is there not to love? I mean, she's cute and all, but what does she have over me? He loves this bomb ass pussy that I have. I've done things with him I have never done with any other man. I am a little ashamed of a lot of memories, especially when I went to Trapeze with him.

Trapeze is an adult club in Atlanta that you can go to and have sex. You can go alone or with a partner. You can even watch. I was so nervous about going to this place, but Eric talked me into going with him. "You sure you're OK about going here," Eric asked? "Yeah, baby, if you want to experience something, I want to experience it with you," I replied nervously. "I got us space there with another couple," he explained. "What does the other couple look like?" I asked, "If I'm going to hook up with them, at least they can look good." Eric showed me a picture of Jim and Keisha. Jim was a tall, dark skin, handsome man that looked like someone who was in corporate. Keisha is the epitome of a goddess. She was gorgeous, with long wavy hair and caramel skin. "I think these two would do just fine," I replied. The atmosphere at trapezes was so erotic; couples were all around making out and having sex. We met with Jim and Keisha in the back after taking off our clothes and putting on a towel. I walked over to introduce myself to them, and I sat in between the couple. Jim slowly came up to me and grabbed me from the back of my neck, and started kissing me softly on my lips. Jim was careful and tender with the soft kisses he planted on my lips and neck. Keisha was in sync with her husband, letting me know this wasn't their first time with another couple. She removed my towel and started kissing me on my breast. She gripped them as she teased each nipple with the tip of her tongue. I looked across the room. Eric was sitting there watching everything take place as he stroked himself in rhythm. The couple both started caressing me and licking me. This made me nervous and turned on at the same time. I had never had a woman touch me and never had two people sex me at the same time. I went through all of this even though it was uncomfortable for me, but Eric loved it. After watching me getting turned out by this couple. Eric joined in and began fucking Keisha from behind as she was sucking my breast, and Jim was sliding in and out of my wet pussy. I started getting a little jealous after hearing Keisha's screams and moans because Eric had never fucked me like that before. Her moans and facial expressions looked like a tormented person from being fucked so well. I wanted that feeling, too. Jim noticed I was more into watching Eric and Keisha than enjoying him. He began pounding into my pussy, and I quickly diverted my attention back to my lover and took every inch. I was in pure ecstasy. After an hour of orgasms, we finished our fuck session. We left the room and went to put on our clothes, and then we said our goodbyes. We all walked to our cars separately, probably never crossing paths again. "Did you enjoy yourself?" Eric asked. "It was different," I added sheepishly. "I'm still not ready to stop," he said. As I looked over to the driver's seat, Eric's dick was still erect and ready for another round. Eric drove the car around a block and pulled over. He looked at me, and I climbed over the seat and mounted his erection. I began giving him all of me as if I would never fuck him again. "Yes, baby, give me all of this good pussy," he moaned. Eric did things to me that night that I had never experienced with any man before. After being with him, no other man could compare. I was his forever, but now this new bitch is ruining everything.

On top of having a four-way with random strangers, Eric and I have had our fair share of drama throughout the past two years. I have caught him with many random women within that short time. One time I saw him eating with the server at Landmark diner, and I walked up and confronted him and her about it. He said it wasn't anything; they were just friends, but I don't believe any of that shit. I have confronted him at work about this one girl named Jessica. He was texting every fucking night, and I may have cost him his job. I really don't care if I did. At the moment, I was just angry. I wasn't thinking about that shitty job that wasn't paying him much. He says I'm jeopardizing him from getting his money together to see his daughter, but I don't see it like that. I just want him to stop fucking these other women and be with me. None of these whores could ever love him as I do. Who would carve his initials on their arm for love? Me, that's who. He thought that was a little extreme, but I think it was my way of showing him we would be together forever. I am just waiting for this Danny chic to kick rocks so that my baby and I will be together.

Why should I be here lonely, and this bitch is over there happy? I got to put a stop to it! Even If I have to physically hurt her. I'm sure Eric is still lying about knowing that it is my calling. Pretty soon, I am going to have to make myself known. Tomorrow night, I will just send her the pictures of him lying naked in my bed that will get her blood boiling. I have to orchestrate my next move carefully because if you want to get a bitch, you have to do a lot of planning. This woman will get this bitch. When I get done with her, she will wish she never met him. The only person who should be with Eric is me, and only me. Until she understands that logic, I will make her life a living hell.

19. Eric

The messed up thing about this situation is that I know who is calling Danny, and I know exactly who vandalized her car. This whole situation has gotten out of hand, and I have to stop it. Trina has absolutely lost her mind. I don't even know if I should go there, but I definitely need to have some words with her. I completely lied to Danny, and I know if she finds out there is someone else and that I know the person who's been harassing her, she will not want to have anything to do with me if she finds out. I can't let that happen. I'm going to have to stop Trina, but I do not know-how. I called my brother to get some ideas about what to do.

My brother Chip is like having a friendly live wire. He seems pleasant and approachable, but if you get too close, he will shock the shit out of you. I know he has done some awful shit in the past. He was a big-time dealer up north, and he was the guy you would call if you wanted someone to disappear. I don't want him involved because Trina might end up in the river. However, I need some advice on how to handle this situation without having to kill this bitch. So I called him. "Hey Chip, what's up," I asked? "Nothing much, man." "What's going on with you?" Chip asked "Man, I got a real messed up situation right now," I said. "What's up, little bro," he asked, sounding very concerned. "Well, I've been dating this chick for a few months now. She's really cool and sexy as hell," I said. "Pretty much everything I want in a woman," I added. "However, I got this psycho bitch I used to mess with who stole a number out of my phone and called her every day," I said. "She followed me last night and vandalized her car," I added. "You have a real-life fatal attraction going on," he laughed. "Yes, I do, bro, and I don't know what to do about it," I said. "You seriously will have to figure out how to get rid of this other chick. You may have to threaten her," he added. "Man, you know I don't put my hands on women," I said. "You may have to do something because this bitch is out-of-control, and you have a serious problem," he said. "If the new chick finds out, you are going to wish you did something," he added. "Especially when she finds out that you have something to do with all the stuff that's happened recently, he said. "She's going to get rid of you quickly," he added. "So, do you need me to do something about it, or do you need me to do something real quick," he said. "You know I will," he added. "No, man, I just need some advice. No mafia shit," I laughed. "Who me? I'm an angel," he said. "Angel of death," I said, laughing. "Well, brother, you have to come up with something soon and really quick," he said. "Call me when you need my help," he added. "Ok, bro, talk to you later," I said. "Ok, brother, love you," he said. "Bye, crazy-ass," I said, laughing. Although my brother had me rolling from our conversations, this was not a laughing matter. He was serious about one thing: this situation needed to be handled. It's been going on too long.

20. A Real Surprise

Today is my first day back at work after a long weekend. I was getting really paranoid after many prank calls, plus the incident with my car. As I was walking from my car today into the building, I swore I was being followed from the parking lot. Maybe it's just a figment of my imagination, but I really feel uneasy about today. I walked into the building, and the first face I saw was Steve with a big smile on his face. "Man, I am so happy to see you," I told him. "I had a very long weekend," I said. "What happened?" Steve asked. "Well, not only do I have a stalker, but I got my windows busted out as well," I added. "What the hell? Is it someone that your boyfriend knows?" Steve asked. "He claims he does not know who has done it, but I suspect he does," I explained. "These things didn't start happening to me until I started talking to him." Well, if he knows, he needs to handle it or say something to you about it," Steve said. "Maybe he's denying it because he's trying to handle it," Steve added. " I thought about that, but at least he could've been honest with me about it from the start. He should have told me instead of having me fear for my safety," I said. "Well, that is true because once you tell one lie in a relationship, you make another lie to cover up the first one," Steve added. 'Well, I don't want to be in a relationship based on lies. The relationship already had a big problem from the get-go," I explained. "Well, if you don't want problems, remember I'm always here," Steve said with the sexiest smile. "Yeah, you are, and the only thing you're doing is making me more confused because I like you too," I said. "Well, you really need to let him go and come over this way," Steve said. "I hear you talking, Steve, and believe me, I'm listening. But I got to see how this goes and then I can go from there," I explained. "If I never met him and met you first, there would be no question. But I've invested months into this relationship, and I can't just jump from one person to the next based on a whim," I said. "I understand, and I never would pressure you, but I want you to know your options are open, and I'm here for you," he whispered as he kissed me gently. "Talk to you later, beautiful woman," Steve said, and he walked away.

I finished my day at work, and at 6 pm, I clocked out and then headed to my car. When I finally reached my car, there was a note on my windshield. I opened the message and read it. The note said he was mine first, with a picture of Eric laying naked next to another woman.

21. The Setup (Danielle)

As I sat in my car, the tears started falling. I am so angry right now, and I feel betrayed. This bastard lied to me! It was someone he knew all along, and now she knows where I work. I am so angry I don't even really want to talk to him or even confront him about it. I just know that I don't want to be with him anymore. If he came into a relationship with another woman and is still married, I can't deal with all that drama. I cranked up my car and headed home. I was deep in thought throughout the entire drive. I finally made it to my destination, and I pulled up to my apartment. I got out of my car and walked to my apartment. A strange woman is sitting on the steps.

My thoughts started racing, and I knew it was her. "May I help you?" I asked. "Yes, you can. Did you get my letter?" she asked. I stopped in my tracks and braced myself. "Oh, so you're the one calling me!" I yelled. "Yes, I am. You're with my man!" Trina yelled back. "Last time I checked, bitch, he has been with me every single day. So, if he's your man, you need to seriously think about your relationship," I told her. Don't get smart with me, bitch. I'm here to tell you personally to back off!" Trina replied. "Look, girl, you don't have to worry about me being in your way anymore. You can have his ass!" I replied. "Well, I've already had him. You just need to leave him alone, and I promise

I won't bother you anymore", Trina said. "Well, you got a deal, but I want him to know that I know about you," I said. "Then you both can stay the fuck out of my life!" I said. "I know you got my number, so call me tomorrow to set up a date so we can all meet up together," I added. "I am sick of this drama. I'm sick of you, and I want to be on my way," I explained. "He needs to know that I know about you and am done with him." Trina bore no expression, but I could feel she was down for this meetup. "I'll call you sometime tomorrow. We have a deal," she said. "Fine with me. Now, get off my steps before calling the cops", I said sternly. "I know you bust out my car windows, and I should have your ass put in jail, but I'm going to let that shit go, and I'm letting Eric and this situation go," I said as I stormed into my apartment.

The tears kept coming as I entered the apartment. I thought this guy would be my knight in shining armor, but he ended up being just another fake. I dried my tears and picked up my phone to call him. He was going to meet me at the coffee shop next to my job tomorrow so I could let him know it was over. "Eric, I got something really important I need to talk to you about," I said. "What is it about?" Eric asked, sounding concerned. "I will talk to you when I see you," I replied. Eric was silent for a moment before he answered, "I will be there, baby." I hung up. There's no reason for me to converse with his ass anymore.

Trina called, and I told her when and where to meet us tomorrow. "I will be there about 4 PM to make sure you're there," I told her. "Oh, I will not miss this for nothing," she replied. After I had set everything up, I started to regret my decision. I did not know what would happen or how all this would turn out. But I need answers from Eric, and I need to move on with my life – without him and his drama.

22. Trina's Revenge (Danielle)

I made it to the coffee shop first and sat down. I got my usual tall, skinny vanilla latte with soy milk. Eric walked in, kissed me on the cheek, and sat down. "What's wrong, baby?" he asked. "Why are you looking so sad?" he added. "I have a lot on my mind, Eric, and really need to talk to you, but I invited someone else, and I'm waiting for them to sit with us", I explained. "Now you have me wondering what's going on," he said, looking very worried. While Eric and I were sitting at the table drinking our cups of coffee in silence, Trina suddenly walked in. She was wearing a bright yellow maxi dress that blended well with her golden-brown skin. Her hair was pulled up with soft curls, highlighting her exotic facial features. She almost looked like a magazine model. I can understand Eric's attraction to her because she is a beautiful woman. As she walks up to the table, you can see the horror on Eric's face. He spoke, puzzled, asking, "What's going on?" "Well, I like you asked that question," I said sarcastically. "It's come to my attention that you had not ended your relationship with Trina when you started a relationship with me," I said. "That's not it," Eric explained. "I've tried to end it with her, but she just won't get the hint." Then, Trina entered the conversation. "You tried to end it to me? But you have been to my house since you've been in a relationship with her," Trina said. "How do you think I got her number from your phone?" I got it while you were sleeping." Eric nervously confessed. " Ok, ok, I admit. I hooked up with Trina once at the beginning of our relationship, " he said. "Then I told her I didn't want to see her anymore." When Trina heard Eric say that, she was about to go ballistic. "Oh, so you just going to end our relationship like that, to be with this bitch!" she yelled. "Hey, wait a minute Trina," I said. "I'm trying to be calm. But you are pushing it, calling me a bitch...BITCH!" Trina peered at me with evil and insane eyes. "You are a simple bitch", she said. "Everything was perfect before you came into the picture. Now he wants to spend time with you, but I promise you both will pay for this shit!," she yelled. "This is not the last time you will see me, and you better watch your fucking backs!" IN a flash, Trina grabbed a cup of coffee and threw it in Eric's face before she stormed out of the coffee shop. Eric yells, "Damn!" He grabs towels and napkins to clean off his face, seeming relieved that the problem is solved. "I promise, baby, I'm so sorry," he pleads. "I have nothing else to do with her," he added. "I don't call her. I don't come by. She has just been stalking me for the last month," he explained. I just looked at him with disgust. "Too little, too fucking late!" I said, fired up about all drama I experienced with him. "If you had been honest with me from the beginning, things could have been different. But I am leaving your ass for good!" I said to him as tears rolled off my cheeks. "Please don't do this. We have a good thing going between us. Everything is perfect. Please don't let this chic mess up our relationship,"Eric pleaded. "No, Eric, you messed up our relationship by not telling me the truth and still going over there to see her when we started talking. You did this, so I'm done and lose my number!," I yelled. "Danny, please do not end it like this. I love you", Eric said with tears in his eyes. I almost felt sorry for him, but my feelings come first, and I do not compromise. "Eric, you have too many issues with yourself. I don't like a lot of drama," I said. "First, it was a wife, and now you have a stalker," I added. "There is no you and me," I said. "I don't want this. I don't want these issues. I just want you to leave me alone," I added. I got up from the table because I just couldn't look at him anymore without wanting to punch him in the face. I walked out of the coffee shop and got into my car. I drove and cried the entire way home. I can't believe I let myself get in this situation, and now I got a crazy-ass bitch threatening to do God knows what to me because of him. I just really don't want anything else to do with him. I just want to be alone. So, Trina, you got your wish.

23. Eric

My life has been spiraling out of control since Danny left. It's been several weeks since I have been texting and calling her, but there is still no response. Trina has been blowing my phone up, showing up at my house and my job, and literally driving me crazy as hell. Everything is my fault because I should've told her the truth. I should've told her I knew Trina was calling and texting her, but I was afraid of losing her. I've already dropped a bombshell on her about being married, and then I would have had to let her know I was still in a completely different relationship with another female. How would that make me look? I would look like a player, but I don't want to be that way anymore. I wanted to be with Danny. I want to spend the rest of my life with her, but now that's over. I need to accept that and move on. On a bright note, I talked to my wife and daughter the other day, and my wife was ready to go along with the divorce. We even talked about trying to co-parent Erica, so I think my plans will be to move back to New York to be with my baby girl. Right now, that's the only important thing, concentrating on raising my daughter.

I am especially ready to get away from this damn lunatic that won't give up on me. Every day, she is constantly calling and texting me. She has shown up to my job making threats, calling me a whore, a dog, a bitch, you name it,

I've been called it. She doesn't understand that she's not the type of woman I want to be with. Yes, the sex is good, and she is a gorgeous woman, but I want someone who can stand for something and not be willing to do anything to please me. I want a woman who can make her own decisions, speak her mind, be independent, have goals, and is trying to make something out of herself in life. All Trina wants to do is party and fuck, and that's not the type of woman I want to spend the rest of my life with. Trina can't seem to understand, and she can't leave me alone. "Ring" Oh my God, the phones are ringing, and I know it's that fool again. "What do you want," I asked, annoyed as hell. "Someone is following me," Trina replied. "You really want me to believe that someone is actually following you, the stalker of the year," I said jokingly. "I don't fucking believe you, and this is ridiculous," I added. "I'm so serious someone has been following me," Trina said. "For a second there, you sound almost convincing," I said. "No, I don't think anyone's following you, ma," I replied. "I think you're just making shit up just for me to come over here to feel sorry for you," I said. "I'm done feeling sorry for you for ruining the best thing in my life, and there's no coming back from it. I don't want to be your friend. I don't want to be nothing to you," I said. All the emotions I have been holding back since my break-up came out at that moment. I have been keeping my feelings inside, but I'm about to unleash them on this crazy ass chick. "Eric, how could you say that to me after all we've been through," she asked. "After all the things I've done to make you happy." "That's just it. I don't want a woman to just do shit to make me happy. I want a woman that is happy with herself," I said. "If you were happy with yourself, you wouldn't even be on the phone with me right now. You will be out enjoying your life and meeting new people, but you keep calling me and harassing me every day just for me to be with you, and you know I don't want you", I added. "So do us a favor and lose my number," I said. "But Eric, listen to me," Trina pleaded. I cut her off. "But Eric, nothing! I'm sick of you. I'm sick of you calling me. Leave me the fuck alone!" I yelled, then hung up. I have been tired of this woman. Now, she's making up lies, telling people she is being followed. If she is being followed, it's probably her guilty conscience because she's so evil. I am done with this shit. I'm done with these women. I'm just going to pack my shit up and head back to New York to be with my daughter fuck them fuck everybody. It's time for me to handle my shit and be the father that my daughter deserves.

24. A New Beginning (Danielle)

The first couple of weeks have been terrible for me. I hate that I got as serious as I did with Eric. I feel like I was such an idiot with this relationship. Why didn't I see the signs? There was no way someone could be randomly calling me and stalking me for no reason. I should've known that it was him. This week, I have been by myself. I really don't want to deal with anything or anything. I gathered up the strength to go to work, but I haven't really gone out since my breakup. I talked to my sisters twice this week, and they've been giving me a little tidbit of encouragement to make me feel better, but I still feel like shit. Steven has been a sweetheart. He will call me every other day and try to see if I need anything, but I just really don't want to bother. Steve is a good guy, and I really like him, but I need time to heal. When the doorbell rings, I am sitting on the couch watching a boring show on TV. I wonder who is at my door this time of day, I thought to myself. I slowly got up to go to the door. It rang again. "I'm coming. Hold up," I announced. I looked through the peephole, and it was a delivery man. The person outside says, "I got a delivery for Danielle Streeter.". I opened the door, and the delivery guy stood with a bouquet. "Thank you," I responded to the delivery guy. I had to see where the flowers came from. If they were from Eric, they're going in the trash as soon as I get in the kitchen. *For someone special, love Steve*. It was from Steve; he is so sweet. I got to call him and tell him thanks. I picked up my cell and dialed Steve. "Hey, you," he said on the first ring. "Hey, how are you?" I answered. "I'm good. The question is how you are holding up," he asked. "I have been better," I responded. "I think I need to get out of the house," I added. "I think you do, too," he replied. "What are you doing tonight?" he asked. "Well, nothing at all," I said. "Well, gather yourself together, get out of that musty robe and get ready for a night out on the town," he laughed. My robe was a little funky since I've been moping around for the past few days, but I didn't tell him that. I walked to my closet and found a cute light blue sundress and some sandals that I hadn't worn yet. I was wary about leaving the house at first, but I think I really needed to get out. As 6 o'clock approaches, I become extra nervous waiting for Steve. I wonder how this night will go because I have been wanting to spend time with him, but I was still in another relationship. Now I'm single I can have some fun. I slipped on my dress and shoes and pulled my hair up in a bun. I applied a light amount of makeup to look as natural as possible but still sexy. I might be in a funk, but I still want to look good. The doorbell rang, and it was Steve standing outside. He was looking exceptionally fine with black jeans and a red polo shirt. He had a fresh cut with Gucci cologne on. Damn, I'm lucky as hell tonight. I know he thought I was crazy because I just stared at him for a few minutes. He broke me out of my daze. "You ok?" he asked, smiling. "Yes, you just look really nice," I replied. "Well, you look beautiful," he replied. We walked out of the apartment to his car. He opened the door for me. "Your chariot awaits," he said with a smile. "Thanks," I replied. "Where are we going?" I asked. "There's a little jazz festival in the park. I thought about getting some dinner first and then listening to a little music,"he said. "That sounds great," I replied. We arrived at the restaurant, and he got out and opened the door for me. We walked in and were seated at a table. "What would you like to eat?" he asked. "I am not picky at all, Steve. That's why I have to run every day", I laughed. "Would you like a little wine with your meal?" he asked. "Sure," I replied. We ordered our dinner and wine. The food here was delicious, and my date was too. He was eating some pasta dish, and he tried to feed me some of his dinner. He was so sweet on the date he listened to me talk about trying to put my life into perspective after this breakup. "I know a breakup can be devastating, but I am and will always be here for you, Danny. You have my heart", he said with the warmest smile. "I know Steve, and you have mine," I replied. "Really," he asked? "Really," I replied. "I always had feelings for you. I was just too stupid to keep talking to Eric," I replied

97

honestly. "I always had my doubts. I think I'm more hurt because I was dumb about the whole thing," I added. "Please stop calling yourself stupid. You are human, and sometimes, as humans, we make mistakes in judging people," he said. "The reality that you are here with me is all that matters." Steve and I wrapped up at dinner as we got ready to head to the park for the jazz festival. We make it to the park, and Steve has a little bag with some wine and blankets for us to sit in the grass. He took out some wine glasses and poured us a glass as I laid the blankets on the grass for us to sit on. We sat down and held hands as we listened to the music play. The concert was really nice, and the music was very relaxing. I look over at Steve, looking sexy.as ever. He tells me how beautiful I am the entire night and how he's so happy to have this opportunity to spend time with me. "I've been waiting for this opportunity too, Steve," I replied. "I wanted to spend time with you for a long time," I added. He leans over, grabs my cheek with his hand, and kisses me. I don't know if it was the wine, but it felt like my body was leaving me like I was floating above myself. Is this what it feels like to kiss someone you love? I don't know, but I think I've fallen in love with this kiss. I moaned into every kiss as he brought me close to him. I never felt like this. It's as if I could be with him forever. I never want him to let me go.

For the next couple of months, I started spending more time with Steve, and my life has been like a dream. We have gone to several movies, dinners, and runs in the park. He has been truly perfect in every way. Every day, I question why I had so much time with Eric. When I could have been happy with Steve. Today he has planned a special dinner at his house. He says he will cook me the best dinner ever, and I can't wait to sample it. He had the place absolutely decked out with roses, candles, and Brian McKnight playing in the background when I arrived. I wore the most provocative sundress I could find in my closet with gold sandals that matched perfectly. I wore my hair loose, and after doing this bomb ass twisted out, my natural curls were popping. "You look exquisite tonight," said Steve. "Thank you, don't look too bad yourself," I replied. He was wearing a black dress shirt with jeans that fit in all the right places. He motioned for me to come to the table, and he pulled out my chair for me to sit down. "I tried to make tonight extra special for you, sweetheart," he said. He brought us to the table and poured us a glass of red wine. The food smelled so good, and the wine was a smooth flavor with a lingering taste of strawberries in my mouth. It was so good I ate every bite. After I wiped my mouth with the napkin, I complimented him on how delicious the dinner was.

I am glad you liked it," he said. "I got a surprise for you," he said, smiling as he pulled out a gift bag that he was hiding on his chair. I opened the bag in pure excitement, and in the bag was a beautiful set of diamond earrings and a necklace with a diamond pendant. "Oh, my goodness, this is beautiful," I screeched. "I'm glad you like it," he said. "Well, the question I wanted to ask tonight's do you want to make things official?" he asked. "I thought I was already your girl," I said, laughing. "Well, I'm a little old-fashioned. I like to ask," he said, smiling from ear to ear. We started kissing, and the next thing I knew, our clothes were all over the kitchen floor. We started making love right there on the kitchen table. Steve was devouring my body, planting kisses in all the right places. He licked and sucked my pussy till I couldn't hold back my moans. My moans got louder and louder. I know his neighbors were getting an earful. I'm sorry, I whispered. "You just feel so good," I moaned. "I would like to make love to you every day," he whispered softly. "You can do whatever you want, Steve, because I'm yours, I replied.

25. Starting Again (Danielle)

Love is such a weird thing. It comes when you least expect it. Everything between Steve and me was great. We would spend every waking moment together. His conversation was so intense to me. I would stare in awe when he spoke like an adolescent little girl, looking at her crush for the first time. He had so many dreams and different ambitions, a quality that I never saw in Eric. He was funny, good-looking, and intelligent. Everything about him was perfect, and I can't even remember the days without him. We would have late-night dinners with burning candles, incense, and soft music in the background. Every time I would see him, I would feel a different intense emotion, like he was the drug and I was an addict. His smell and his touch were intoxicating. I am deeply and completely in love.

Steve and I have dated for a while now. I'm so glad I broke away from Eric's toxic relationship. It was too many issues and too many people involved, and I got to where I was done. Bitches damaging my cars and stalking me. I felt like something terrible would happen, and I did not want to be involved with that. I've never been with a guy who had a stalker. It was next-level bullshit. That girl Trina was utterly out of her mind. Although I believe Eric was done with her at that point, I couldn't trust him anymore, and I was ready to move forward. I couldn't deal with the fact he lied. So right now, I'm happy. I'm in love, and I finally have some stability. I finally get to deal with somebody on my level, and I enjoy every minute.

26. The Breaking point (Danielle)

2 months later ...

I headed home from running two miles around Stone Mountain, and my mind was in deep thought. There were 10 missed calls from Eric when I checked my messages. I just put my phone down. I seriously don't have time for this at all. He hasn't heard from me in a while. At first, he was calling every day and leaving messages. Then the calls slowed down to a few calls a week to none. Maybe he got back with Trina, but he wasn't my problem anymore. I have been going out with Steve for the past nine months. He is so sweet and genuine and has been a good friend to me. I have never been as happy as I have been with Steve. I could never risk what I got with Steve and take Eric back, and I seriously don't want to. I have been thinking about it, and I really think I was in love with good sex. Damn, the sex was fantastic! However, we really had little in common, and I can't deal with liars. I am in the best place in my life right now. No drama, no crazy stalkers, just love. I got out of my car and walked to my apartment when I had a strange feeling I was being followed. "Danny!" The voice yelled. It was Eric. "Oh shit, what the hell does he want? I thought. "I was hoping I would find you," said Eric. "I have nothing to talk to you about," I said. "Please hear me out, Danny," he said. "I just wanted to make peace with you,." he added. "I am headed to New York in a few days. He explained he was moving back to help raise his daughter after his divorce. "I am so happy for you. She needs you there with her," I replied. "I know, and I will be the best dad for her," Eric said. "You will, and I know how much you love her," I said. "I really do," he said. "I just hope you find the happiness you are looking for, Eric," I said. "Are you happy, Danny?" Eric asked. "Yes, Eric, I am thrilled. Thanks for asking", I said. "That's good. I am glad you found the happiness you deserve. "I only want the best for you," he said with a soft smile. His eyes showed the opposite of his smile. I saw sadness in his eyes and disappointment. "Well, can I have a hug," he asked? "Sure," I replied. I reached out to hug him, and suddenly I heard a loud bang! Then I felt something hot searing through my shoulder. I looked at Eric, and blood covered his face as he jumped in front of me. I heard another loud bang stripping through the air, then darkness crept over me, and all I could hear were faint screams all around me.

27. Next day

I whispered, "Where am I?" "Hey, sweetheart," Steven replied softly. "You are in the Hospital," he added. I asked, "What happened?" "According to bystanders, you were talking to Eric on the sidewalk, and someone drove by and shot both of you," Steve explained. "You were lucky that Eric jumped in front of you, that it only grazed you on your side, but Eric wasn't that lucky," Steve explained with sadness in his eyes. I yelled, "What happened to Eric?" "Tell me, Steve," I demanded. Even though Eric and I broke up months ago because of his cheating and lies, I wasn't that heartless, and on that day, he actually apologized for his actions. "They shot him 4 times, once in his arm and 3 times in his abdomen", Steve whispered. "He is on life support, and it doesn't look good, Danny," Steve reluctantly added. He was more afraid of how I would react to this news. I could see the fear in his eyes when he told me the news. Tears slowly crept from my eyes from the realization that Eric may lose his life to protect mine. "I didn't know what to say," I whimpered. "Steve, I don't want him to die," I said between sobs.

Steve looked away and responded, "I know, baby, I know."

A million things ran through my head while I lay in that bed. Was that woman that obsessed with Eric that she would try to kill us both? He was finally moving forward with his life and ready to be with his little girl, and someone came and almost took both of our lives because he couldn't keep his dick in his pants. I almost lost my life because of his mistakes. I just found myself, just learned to love a person who actually loved me in return. Steve was a beautiful blessing to me. He was someone who awakened my heart and my desires all at once. I almost lost that forever.

28. Lavonna

Today, I received a call from the hospital that I needed to head to Atlanta because my estranged husband had just been shot. I asked, "Are you sure it's Eric?" "Yes, and he is in critical condition, and have you listed as his emergency contact," a nurse said calmly on the other end. "Ok, I'm on my way," I said. I almost went into hysterics. I quickly got myself to go to the hospital to check on my estranged husband. I didn't tell anyone that I was already in Atlanta and had been here for a few weeks. So, I took a minute to get there so it wouldn't look suspicious. To be honest, I really didn't feel any way about his condition. Eric and I have been fighting for a while now over custody of our daughter, Erica. He told the court that I was an alcoholic and an unfit mother. I may have a few drinks now and then, but I don't think I'm that bad. Eric, however, made me look like a complete monster to the judge, and we were only a few days away from our next court date. Now he's almost dead in the hospital for being the biggest whore in Atlanta. I don't feel sorry for him at all. He has had a crazy stalker following him for almost a year now, so I'm sure the authorities are all on her ass. The bad thing is the woman he was talking to got hit. She had cut his stupid ass off months ago, so I wondered why he was with her. All I know is I don't care if his ass makes it or not, I just want to keep my daughter, and with Eric fighting for his life in the ICU, things are looking up for me.

29. Trina

This has been a crazy few weeks. Every day when I walk home, it feels like someone is following me. This is not the first time this has happened because a few weeks after Eric ended the relationship with that bitch, someone was following me then. I tried to tell Eric but he didn't want to talk to me. I know it's crazy, or maybe its my conscious getting the best of me for fucking with Eric and that bitch. I admit I may have taken things too far, but I eventually backed off because they broke up and shit. My goal was accomplished! I hope he feels like shit for how he did me. I hope he's hurting like I was.

Ring Ring. I rushed to pick up my phone off of the countertop. Hello, may I be of service? I answer. As the voice talked, I stood there frozen in place. "Please don't tell me this is true!" I screamed. My friend Jamie calls me to tell me that Eric has been shot. I was so upset I dropped my plate of dinner on the floor. The plate shatters into a million pieces. This can't be happening right now! How could this have happened to him? I am so shaken by the news my whole body trembles. I yelled, "How could this have happened, and who could have shot him?"

Knock Knock. Who could that be at my door? I wasn't expecting anyone. I dropped the phone and slowly walked to my door. When I looked out the peephole, I saw two men in black suits. One was black, very tall, handsome, and very young. The other man was Caucasian with a very stocky build, average height, and tanned.

Who's there?" I asked. "Katrina Cook," he asked, looking unsure of himself. "I am detective Rodgers, and this is detective Davis," the handsome one of the two said. "We need you to come with us to the precinct to answer a few questions about Eric Slater's shooting today," Rodgers demanded. "I have been at home all day," I explained. "I hope you don't think I have anything to do with this," I replied. "That's great, Miss Cook, but we need you to come to the station with us. You are not under arrest. We just need you to answer some questions," the officer stated. I agreed and followed them out the door. A thousand thoughts flooded my mind on the drive over there. Will they think I was the shooter because I was stalking him? I threatened them both in a public place. Did anyone see me? I may go to prison for something I didn't do because I was being stupid over a guy that didn't want me. I am seriously fucked right now and might need to call my attorney. I also need to let the police know that someone has been following me. They will not believe me.

I walked into the police station with the officers, and they promptly took me to the interrogation room. "Hello, Miss Cook, I am Detective Rodgers, and this is Detective James. We want to ask you a few questions," he said. "Where were you yesterday around 5 PM?" he asked. "I was at home. I just got off work, and I went directly home," I replied. He asked, "Do you have anyone that can say that you were home?" "Well, my neighbor saw me go into the apartment because I talked to her for a few minutes outside," I replied. The other detective asked, "So if we talk to your neighbor, she can tell us you were at home around 5 o'clock?". "Yes, because I actually stopped outside her door before stepping foot into my apartment," I replied. I started asking, "What is this about? Do you think I actually shot them?" "Yes, I do because, according to Miss Streeter, she was being stalked by you for a minute, putting you as the prime suspect," he retorted. "OK, I know I made a few phone calls, and I harassed her, but I never would kill anyone or try to kill anyone. I just wanted them to break up, and after they did just that, I backed off," explained. "You backed off, but before you backed off, you did a lot of crazy shit. Am I right?" he asked. "Yes, I was a little upset about the breakup, and yes, I did crazy things, but there is no way I would shoot Eric. I really cared about him a lot, and it devastated me when I heard the news," I said with tears in my eyes. "I'm still pretty shaken up about the whole thing because I swear someone has been following me now," I added. "I called Eric yesterday to tell him I thought I was being followed, but he didn't believe me," I said. The detective asked with concern, "How long have you noticed someone following you?" "It's been about a few weeks," I said. "I just have this feeling that I'm being followed, and I don't can't see anybody, but something just is not right," I added. "One evening, I came to my apartment, and some of my things seemed out of place. Someone was in my apartment, but I brushed it off because I thought maybe I was tired and just seeing things," I explained. "However, later, I noticed my spare key was missing. I asked the landlady to change the locks, but she will not get the locksmith there next week," I added. "Well, we will check into this and check with your landlord and your neighbor to make sure your story adds up," Rodgers replied.

30. Detective Rodgers

I really didn't believe this chick's story, so my partner and I went to her apartment with my partner to check out her story. She lived in a quiet area next to Midtown, and we arrived at her apartment building around 2:00 p.m. We walked up the stairs to her apartment complex, and we realized that there were cameras everywhere, so this camera footage may give us some clues. We went to her neighbor's apartment and knocked on the door. She promptly opens. "Hello, Miss Smith, I am Detective Rodgers, and this is Detective James, and we have a few questions for you," I stated. She asked, "Are you all coming by to ask me about the strange woman who has been coming around the building?" No, I actually wanted to talk to you about an attempted murder investigation," I replied. "Where were you around five yesterday evening?" I asked. "I was probably about an hour outside talking to Miss Trina," she replied. "OK, and you're absolutely sure," I asked. "Yeah, I talked to her for an hour, probably more than that. We always stand outside and talk about what went on throughout the day and other things," she said. "Trina doesn't have any friends to talk to and mostly stays to herself," she added. "We also talked about the strange woman around the building, and Miss Trina was concerned if someone was following her." "Yes, she mentioned that to us today," I replied. "Do you

113

know who has access to these cameras in your building?" I asked. "Yes, those cameras are on at all times," she said. "The apartment manager has access to those cameras," she added. "OK, thank you so much, and we appreciate your cooperation," I said. "So this story about someone following her is actually something," I said. "Yeah, I thought she was pulling our leg," James replied. "'Well, let's go to the leasing office and check and see if we can see anything on the cameras," I said.

Walking to the apartment complex office, an old woman was sitting at the desk. The wrinkles in her face told her life story of pain that accented her very thick rim glasses and salt and pepper hair. "Good evening, officers," she said pleasantly. "How can I help you?" she asked. "Well, ma'am, we are investigating a case, and we were told by some of your tenants there was a strange woman around the building," I said. "Do you know anything about that?" I asked. "No, I have heard nothing about a strange woman, but I have video cameras set up all around the building, so if anyone was trespassing, it would catch them on video," she replied. She asked calmly, "Would you like to see the videos?" "Yes, ma'am, that would be very helpful," I responded. She promptly walked to another room where cameras and TV were set up. She went through the videos of last week. You can catch a small frame woman in view in one video, walking in the hallway. You can tell this woman had a light complexion, but she had a hat on her head, so it was hard to see her hair color. She appeared to walk past Trina's door on one video several times. In the video, at the end of the week, she seems to break into Trina's apartment to stay there for at least an hour and come out.

"So I'll be damned, she wasn't lying. Someone was stalking the stalker," I said. "Where do they do that?" James said, laughing. "Apparently here," I replied. "So now we got an attempted murder stalker situation. This shit gets better by the minute," I said. "Yeah, this is such a crazy situation. I don't even know what to think anymore," James responded. "Well, we got a look into who this chick is and who else this guy Eric was dealing with to find out what really happened." "Time to dig deep, James," I added. "I already brought the shovel," he replied. "Hey, don't you think we need to warn the young lady?" he added. "Yes, let's call her," I replied.

31. Danielle

I stayed in the hospital for at least two days. Doctors tell me that Eric is still in the ICU, fighting for his life. I really can't believe that all of this is happening. It's like a bad dream, but Steve was here with me throughout everything, and I love him so much for that. I was looking for something in Eric when Steve was there in front of me all this time. I can genuinely see myself spending the rest of my life with him. However, first things first, we need to find who shot us. The whole time, I thought it was this crazy bitch Trina. This psycho has been stalking us for the past couple of months. I did notice, however, that once we broke up, she backed off. I guess she got what she wanted, Eric, without me. The detectives came in today and talked to me about the case, and, to my surprise, they really didn't think it was Trina. They are sure that it is someone else because someone is now stalking Trina. What goes around comes around, but this is actually scary. What if this person tried to go after me again? If they thought, Trina did nothing, and they admitted to seeing another person break into her apartment.

If that's the case, she needs to be really careful because she may be next.

32. Steve

Everything has been completely crazy for the past few days. The love of my life is lying in the hospital bed because she was dating a guy with too many issues. I don't know why the fuck she was with him that day, but she swears he walked up on her. Why doesn't this dude just give up? He had a perfectly good woman in front of him, and he blew it! This dude has a wife and an extra girlfriend. What the fuck? My love could have been dead because of his shitty choices. Wait a damn minute, he has a wife. Why aren't they investigating her? She should have been the first one they looked at. Danny told me they have been going through a really messy divorce. That's enough motivation to kill him. I will call Danny and tell her she needs to let the detectives know this info. She may be the one who shot at them. I'm praying that they catch who did this because I am scared for Danny, and I will let nothing happen to her as long as I'm breathing. The woman I want to share my life with is this one. I was planning on getting a ring this week for her before all this sit happened. I know this may move too quickly because we have only been together for 2 months as a couple, and 6 months as friends, but I can't see myself with no one but Danny.

33. Katrina

I took a shower after coming home from the precinct. Being with common criminals made me feel dirty. I know I was wrong for all the dirty shit I did to Eric and Danny, but I was really hurt. How could he leave me like that? I am God's gift to men. I mean, look at me, I am a bad bitch. Why was he so hooked on her? Well, that was the past, I made sure of. I don't think she would ever attempt to go anywhere near that bitch since whoever tried to take a shot at him. Is still out there. If I were her, I would be terrified.

I finally made it up the hall to my apartment. Home sweet home, I silently mumbled to myself. When I put my key into the apartment door, I noticed it was unlocked. Damn, did I leave it open when I rushed off with those cops? Shit, I can't remember at all. I strolled into my apartment and looked around. My apartment looks ok, I said to myself. This new stalker got me spooked as hell. Get your shit together, Trina, I thought to myself. After hanging up my jacket and turning on my bath water, I head to my bathroom. I poured some of my lavender bubble baths into the water. Man, I'm going to enjoy this relaxation, I said to myself. I slowly pulled my shirt over my head and turned around. That's when I saw her.

34. Lavonna

"Well, well, Mr. Eric, all your games have finally caught up," I whispered as I stood over Eric in the hospital, struggling for his life. I felt somewhat bad for his situation, but not bad enough to shed a tear. He has been giving me hell with this custody battle. He claims I am an alcoholic drug addict. So far from the truth, I never did drugs in my life. I just like an occasional drink after work. I don't see what's wrong with that. It's not like I can't stop when I'm ready. He made me seem like a monster in court, saying I was abusive. I grew up getting spankings, and I turned out ok. If my child disobeys me, I'm going to lay my hands on her. She needs to learn to obey me. I have occasionally left a bruise here or there, but she shouldn't be so damn pale like her dad. Actually, I really hate that she looks like him. Her eyes, complexion, and curly hair are like her dad's, but she is my daughter. He is not just going to take her from me. He will never take her from me. I will make sure his life is pure hell, and he will understand that some of his actions in life have deadly consequences. "Excuse me, Miss," a young nurse said as she walked in, trying to get my attention. "Yes," I said. "Are you his wife?" she asked. "Yes, I am," I answered boastfully. "Well, some detectives were here earlier wondering if you had come by, and I told them no," she said. "Thank you for letting me know. I think I will leave for a while to let my sweet hubby get his rest", I said.

35. Detective Rodgers

We attempted to call Trina several times but got no answer, so we headed to the apartment. To our horror, someone made it there first. The apartment was in disarray, and there were blood splatters everywhere. We looked around the place and discovered Trina's lifeless body in the doorway between the bathroom and the bedroom. This individual has a revenge thing going on, I thought. I genuinely don't feel this is a random break-in because nothing valuable was missing. We inspected every inch of the residence, dusting for fingerprints and any clue that the culprit could have left behind. "I spotted a bloody footprint, partner," James yells from the front of the apartment. "Well, someone has made a mistake and left behind a clue," I replied. "That's not surprising," retorted James. "You see it often when a person kills out of anger. They always seem to make a mistake," James added. "Well, we learn now that Miss Trina here is innocent," I responded. "Too bad the perpetrator got to her first," I added. "Yes, this was an absolutely senseless murder and whoever we are dealing with is a very dangerous individual," responded James. "Well, we'll have to promptly get forensics to check for fingerprints and any more clues left behind," James added. "This day is certainly going to shit," I exclaimed. "We're not getting any closer to who did everything. All we know is that it's a woman, but who is this woman?" I asked. "We can't question the guy, Eric, because he is still in a coma, so we undoubtedly need to look into his history," replied James. "We need to call Miss Danielle and get more information about him," I said. "Yeah, I think that's a good idea," agreed James.

Hello, Miss Danielle, this is Detective Rodgers. I got a few questions to ask you, and I'm making it pretty quick," I said. "First, I have to deliver you some awful news, I explained. I added that the woman Trina was just found dead in her apartment," I added. "I can't actually go into details, but it appears to be foul play," I continued. "I need you to keep this information I'm giving you between us, but is there any other woman involved with Eric," I asked her. "Well, he was married," Danielle said. "That was the other reason I dumped him," she added. "What the fuck? You gotta be kidding me? Married?" I thought. "Do you know her name?" I asked. "Yes, I do. It's Lavonna, and they were going through a serious custody battle," Danielle explained. "He was trying to get legal guardianship of his daughter, but his wife lives in New York. At least I assume she is,"she added. "Well, we need to check into this and figure out if she's in New York or Atlanta, committing these crimes," I explained. "Just stay on standby and be safe," I added. "I will, but I will be released from the hospital soon, and this news is actually scaring me," Danielle whispered.

"Well, we're working to see if we can have you put on police surveillance for the time being because this person is very dangerous, and our job is to keep you safe," I reassured her. "I will talk back to you soon," I said. Thanks for the information," I added. "No problem," Danielle responded.

"I can't understand why the hospital never told us he had a wife,"I exclaimed. "Well the nurses at the desk stated she only came to visit twice," said James. "I wonder why we are just hearing of this?" I asked. "I don't know but someone really dropped the ball on this one, I will be having a word with the ICU supervisor," I said angrily. " We could have found her at the beginning of this investigation", I added.

36. The Revelation (Danielle)

Now I wonder if the wife's involved. Finding out the crazy bitch Trina is dead is mind-blowing. I'm terrified for myself and Eric because if she knows he is still alive, she may come to the hospital to finish the job? If she killed the other girl, what would she do to me? I have to call Steve and inform him of what's going on because I can't do this shit on my own. This is just too much. Eric had a bunch of shit going on, and I don't even understand why he didn't assume his wife was this crazy. You never realize who you're dealing with until shit hits the fan. I didn't think she'd go this far, but she was adamant about not giving up custody. Hopefully, before she knows our location, the police will find her.

Steve picks up on the first ring. "Hey sweetie, how are you today?" Steve asked. "I'm not doing so well. Steve, I just found out this alarming news from the cops," I replied. "What is it?" Steve asked. "They told me that the crazy bitch is dead; someone murdered her and has been following her days before it happened," I explained. "Well, who do they assume it may be?" he asked. "The detectives speculate the person of interest is his estranged wife," I replied. "They were going through a nasty custody battle, and he was getting custody of his daughter," I continued. "The detective suggests the ordeal gave her just enough motivation to come and kill him," I added. "Yeah, a custody battle would definitely give someone motive, so you may be still in danger," Steve replied. "The cop mentioned they're setting up surveillance at my home to make sure she didn't retaliate against me," I said. "Trina's murder shows that this individual is crazy and dangerous," I added. "Eric got himself in real serious shit," Steve replied. "I mean, having one crazy stalker and one crazy wife is extreme, " Steve said. "Danielle, in all honesty, you would have been more involved in this shit if you hadn't let him go when you did," Steve said seriously. "Yeah, I was thinking about that too," I replied. "Well, maybe this shit will end soon, and they catch her, " Steve said. "I hope so too because I'm terrified," I added. "You never have to be scared if you got me because I'm going to make certain you're protected and nothing ever happens to you again," declared Steve. "Sweetheart, that's why I love you so much," I exclaimed.

37. Going Home (Danielle)

They released me from the hospital today. Steve was there with the wheelchair, waiting to take me to the car. "Your chariot awaits, my dear," he said with the biggest smile. "I can't wait to get home to cuddle with you, baby," I said, smiling seductively. "I might hurt a little, but I know what would take all that pain away, a little of Steve." He carefully took me to the car and helped me inside. He walked to the other side and jumped into the driver's seat. I looked back at the hospital as we drove off. So many thoughts race through my head. I wondered if Eric would pull through. I wondered if the perpetrator was still out there, and I asked if she would come after me next. When I arrived at my place, I was terrified. Although Steve was holding my arm as I walked in, I couldn't help but feel helpless. "I'm going to fix you something nice to eat, run your bath water, and cover that wound on your shoulder so it won't get wet," Steve announced. "Thanks, baby. I am so lucky to have my own personal nurse to pamper me," I said. "I will do whatever you want me to do, beautiful woman. I am just glad that you are home," he said. "I will do whatever it takes to get you well," he added. "I am glad you are here with me," I responded. We ate a delicious meal he prepared for me and talked for hours. I missed being this close to him and kissing him. He washed my body as we sat in the water together. The water running down to my breast as he caressed me from behind made my whole body tingle with excitement. I turned slightly and kissed his waiting lips. "I want you tonight, Steve. I know you are scared to hurt me, but it's just my shoulder," I pleaded. "My pussy works just fine, and it's about time you had some dessert after that delicious meal you cooked," I added. "Can I taste it?" He asked teasingly. "You can taste all of me if you like," I answered. Steve helped me out of the tub and carefully dried me off while he kissed each part of my body at the same time. "How does that feel?" he asked. "It feels amazing," I whispered. Steve walked me to the bed and carefully laid me down. He put light kissing on my lower thighs and moved up to my inner thighs. He licked and sucked my pussy as if he was starving for it. I moaned with every kiss as he caressed my ass and pulled my body closer to his mouth. "Oh, Steve, this is amazing," I moaned. "Glad you like it because I got more," he responded. He carefully turned me to the side of my good shoulder and got behind me. "I'm trying to make sure I don't hurt that shoulder," Steve whispered. "I understand, baby, but I need you inside me right now," I moaned softly . He slowly pushed his manhood into my juicy, awaiting lips, and I moaned from the pleasure it brought. We made love to each other all night and until sunrise. It was the most fantastic night, and I was beyond satisfied.

The next morning, I woke up to have breakfast in bed. "Thank you, honey," I said. "Anytime, baby, and only for you," Steve said. "Steve, I am so grateful to have you," I said with tears in my eyes. "I am so sorry that my life has been so messy, even after stepping away from my relationship with Eric," I added. "You didn't have control of that," Steve said. "Please don't beat yourself up about it," He added. "How could you have possibly known you would run into Eric that day and someone was following him? Eric is really in a dangerous situation right now and is still fighting for his life", Steve said in a serious tone. "I hope things will come around for the guy, especially with him trying to do the right thing for his daughter," Steve added. "Me too," I replied. "Well, finish eating, dear; we have a hectic day today," Steve said jokingly. "What are we doing today?" I asked. "Binge-watching some movies," Steve replied. "There is cuddling involved," he added. "Oh yes, anything for cuddling," I replied, laughing.

38. Detective Rodgers

I have tried to reach Eric's estranged wife for several days with no luck.This was strange for a person who's husband has been shot. Normally they would contact the station first. I contacted some family members of Lavonna, but they only knew that she came to Atlanta once he got shot. They were not aware of her whereabouts before then. She left her daughter in the care of her mother several days before the shooting, so she could have been to Atlanta before the shooting. All I know is this is a hard woman to get in contact with. After I checked the records at the hospital, and found out that she visited him twice, Her whereabouts since then have been a mystery. She had an excellent motive to hurt him because she was about to lose her daughter, and from what I was told, she didn't work, so the child support kept her afloat. We're going to have officers just hang out at the hospital if she shows up again. I checked her police record in New York, and she had a couple of DUIs, and I was told that she was in and out of rehab for drinking. The court documents stated she was trying to remain sober to keep her daughter. Eric's record was clean, so it looked better for him than hers. I just hope we find her soon before anything else happens. Miss Streeter is on watch in case she tries to hurt her. I also got officers at the hospital to look out for her if she tries to show up to harm him while he's in recovery. I just hope something breaks soon so that we can close this case.

39. Lavonna

This detective is really getting on my fucking nerves. He keeps calling around and asking my family members where I'm at. He ought to know that I'm in Atlanta, especially after I got called to come to the hospital. I don't understand why he won't just back off. If he knew what kind of person Eric was, he would feel sorry for me and my situation. I have been through a lot throughout the many years' Eric and I were together. Eric and I met back when I was attending Georgia State University. We were originally from New York, so we hit it off right away. We were in a few classes together my freshman year, and it was love at first sight for me. He had the most gorgeous smile, and his body was like looking at a male model in one of those GQ magazines. He was sexy with the personality to go with the package. We would go to the park some days and lay on the grass to talk for hours. His dreams were my dreams, and I wanted to spend every waking minute with him. We had plans to get married and stay in Atlanta. I was all for it. I would do anything to make this man happy, but my parents weren't too happy about me not returning to New York after college. Then the rumors about Eric started when I was a junior. Some females would claim that they were dating Eric. Some would even approach me and confront me about him. I tried to ignore them because I knew Eric was my soulmate and had my own little secret.

"I'm pregnant, Eric," I said excitedly. "You are what? "he answered in shock. "I am having our child," I explained. "Well, baby, I'm shocked, but I am happy, and I will be the best dad ever," He exclaimed. "I am so happy to hear you say that, baby," I said. The 9 months were tough, and I had a hard time trying to go to my classes anymore. I was sick almost every day, and Eric was normally out with his friends throughout most of my pregnancy. The rumors of him with other girls got too much to handle, and I confronted him about it. "Are you with other women, Eric? "I asked him. "No, Lavonna, I am only with you," he answered. "So, who is this?" I asked, showing him a picture of him with another girl. I had my girls Teri and Sheila following him around for months. They spotted him out with this girl in our chemistry class last semester. He had been sneaking out to see her since I was pregnant. Once he saw the picture, he had no choice but to tell the truth. "Yes, baby, but I promise I am not seeing her anymore," he pleaded. Little did I know things were about to worsen after the baby arrived.

Erica Renae Slater was born on September 13, 2012. She was an 8lbs 12oz beautiful baby girl. Eric was in love with her from the day she arrived. She was like the mirror image of him, only cuter. He was a wonderful father to her and made sure that we spoiled her like a little princess. We got married two months after Erica was born. It wasn't anything special; it was a quick courthouse wedding, but we were official. After we got married, things seemed to get a little better, but Eric went right back to cheating. A few months and a few years of dealing with it, I started drinking every evening after I got off work. My drinking did get out of control, and our fights got a little crazy. Eric told me that he would be done with the relationship if I didn't stop drinking. He was done with the relationship a long time ago.

Once he told me he didn't want to be with me anymore and wouldn't stop cheating, I moved back to New York with my baby to live with my parents. All my dreams, school, and everything had gone down the drain. This put me into a deeper depression when I hid my drinking problem from my parents. They found out after I got a few DUI's and lost my job. This news gave Eric enough ammunition to file for full custody of Erica. Eric will not have full custody of my daughter. She is my life, and I don't think I can even survive without her. So as far as Eric getting shot. He got what he deserved, her ass got what she deserved, and any other female bitch around him deserved it. Now, because of this detective bitch, the hospital is on lock, and I can't even go to visit without getting questioned. Little do they know I got a bigger plan, and they can't be everywhere.

Today I found out where Miss Fancy pants lived. Eric was so in love with her that he wasn't willing to work things out with me. What did she have that I didn't have? She didn't even want his ass anymore, and he was still following her around like a lovesick puppy. He is not shit, and he needs to feel the hurt and pain I do. He will not take my daughter from me! That's my fucking kid!

40. Eric

If anyone says getting shot is a breeze, they lied. I've been out of my coma for a week and in recovery. The hospital has to keep everything under wraps because of the circumstances, and only the detectives may know I'm actually awake. The doctor told me that my trach would be removed today, and I would begin physical therapy and speech therapy as soon as possible. Detectives came to the hospital today to talk to me about the developments in my shooting. They informed me Danielle was doing great and that the bullet only grazed her. They also told me the awful truth about what happened to Trina and that she was murdered. Now, I know she wasn't the one that shot us. Plus, the last time I talked to Trina, she pretty much let me know she was done, and she was just happy that Danielle and I broke up.She also told me that she was being followed but I didn't believe her. Trina just wanted to make sure I was just unhappy as she was, and she ruined any chances I had with Danielle. Danielle deserved more than I could ever give her. I am happy that she is safe, and I wish only the best for her, even if I have to let her go. I have too much going on to bring my drama into someone's life.

For the past few months, I've been going through a custody battle with my crazy ass wife and trying to complete the divorce. Oh my God!

Could Lavonna have done this? I know she was furious with me and adamant about not giving up my daughter, but would she go to this extreme? I seriously hope it wasn't her, for Erica's sake. I'm willing to work with Lavonna if she's ready to go into rehab and get some help for her drinking problem. The last time I talked to her, she wasn't hearing anything I had to say. She doesn't even have a problem,according to her. As long as she doesn't fix this, she doesn't need to be around my daughter, subjecting my little girl to her addiction. I just hope that they remove my trach soon so I can talk to the officers. I may need to tell them about Lavonna. According to the nurses, I know Lavonna has been here to see me twice, but because I was still in a coma, I don't remember it. If she wanted to kill me, then why didn't she try then? Maybe she thought I was going to die, anyway. I really hope that Danielle is safe because I could live with myself if anything happened to her. I know I messed things up with her, but I really loved her. Hopefully, I will recover soon to get out of this hospital and move on with my life. The detectives really need to find out who did this to me, so they won't come back and try again.

41. A Dangerous Game (Danielle)

Tonight I'm home alone. Steve had to pick up a shift at the hospital. There are cops outside watching my home, but I need to go to the store. I feel like a trapped bird in a cage. I mean, really, why would his wife want to bother me, anyway? Eric and I broke up a while ago. So she shouldn't be an issue. I'm going to get my purse and head my ass to the store. I don't think I will be in danger at the grocery store. I went to my bathroom and took a nice, warm shower. Got out and put on some sweatpants and an Auburn T-shirt. I grabbed my purse off the bed and headed to my car for a fun-filled night at the grocery store. An officer stopped me before I could get in the car. "Where are you headed, Miss Danielle?" the officer asked. He was a nice build, a little younger than me, with some maturity in his eyes. "Just to the grocery store. I have nothing to snack on here, and I just want to get out and get some air," I replied. "Do you need us to follow you to the store?" he asked?. "No, I think I'll be OK. I really need someone to stay here to make sure no one gets in my house," I replied . "OK, Miss Streeter, I will do," he stated, like he was taking an order from a drill sergeant. I slowly got in my car and cranked it up to listen to some R-&-B classics. After pulling out of the driveway, I headed up the road to Kroger's. I got out of my car and walked up to the store. As soon as I got in, I grabbed my cart and just went from aisle to aisle, trying to find some snacks and something to cook at the house. As I walked down the different aisle, I had an uneasy feeling that someone was following me, but I shook it off. Don't start being paranoid, Danielle, I said to myself. The more anxious I got, the quicker I walked down the aisles. As soon as I got everything I needed, I headed to the register. When I reached the cash register, a woman was standing behind me that looked familiar, but I wasn't sure where I had seen her before. "Is this all for you?" Miss Lady, the cashier said to me, smiling. "Yes, I got to head back home. There were a few things I needed at the house, because I was almost out of everything," I explained. "I understand," the cashier said. "I work at the grocery store, and I forget to bring stuff home all the time, so you're not the only one," the cashier said, laughing. I took out my wallet to pay with my credit card for my items, and while I was swiping my card, I noticed that the lady behind me was staring at me really hard. I hurried and signed my receipt and shook off the uneasy feeling. I left the store and quickly headed to my car. Before I could get to my car fast enough, the lady at the register was quickly walking toward me. She spoke to me when she caught up to me. "Hey, how are you doing?" she asked. "I'm doing fine. I'm just trying to get home", I replied. "Where do I know you from?" she said. "I'm not sure," I answered as I frantically looked for my keys in my purse. At this moment, I really started feeling uneasy talking to this lady. "You know we all have a twin somewhere", she said with a menacing grin. I quickly turned to put my groceries in the car, and I noticed her walking up really close, too close to me. All of a sudden, I started getting lightheaded. "What the fuck did you do to me?" I asked right before everything went black.

When I woke up, I was in the backseat of my car. "What the fuck just happened?" I asked. "You don't need to be asking questions, bitch. I ask them," she said with a menacing snarl. "I don't know what you want from me. If it's money, you can use one of my cards," I said with tears welling up in my eyes. "I don't want your cash. I just want you to feel the same pain I'm going through,"she said. I immediately knew my kidnapper's identity. "Oh my God, you are Eric's wife!" I screamed. "Bitch, calm your ass down. Before I have to shoot your ass again!"she yelled. I noticed the 9mm on the passenger seat, but my hands were tied, so I couldn't reach it. "Why are you doing this? I'm not with Eric's cheating ass!", I explained. "I want him to suffer when he hears his precious Danny is dead," she said, laughing as she drove us to her hotel.

42. Steve

I got off work a little early and realized I hadn't heard from Danny. I headed to her house. The police detectives were outside when I pulled up. "What is going on?" I yelled. "Ms. Streeter hasn't returned home after going to Kroger's," the officer replied. "The surveillance cameras at the Krogers show an unidentified female dragging Danny to the backseat of her own car and driving off," he added. "Little do she know we asked Ms. Streeter to keep a tracker in her purse until we found the perpetrator," Detective Rogers said. "Sir the car is dinging only 2miles away. We have officers set up in the area waiting for her,"James said.

"How could y'all let her leave the house? What the fuck are y'all here for" I screamed. "Ms. Streeter demanded us not to chaperone her to the store," the detective explained. "I think she felt we would always know where she is with the tracker," the detective added. "Hey, Detective James, they got eyes on her," an excited officer screamed. "Ok, guys, let's rock and roll. We gotta get this criminal", commanded Detective James. The officers raced out of the driveway and demanded that I stay here at the house. All kinds of crazy thoughts ran through my head about my girl. "I can't lose her now," I mumbled to myself. She is my everything. I hate she was ever involved with this Eric dude, and I wish all this drama was over. I slowly grabbed my things and headed towards the house, feeling helpless.

43. Detective Rodgers

The tracker in her purse led us to a rundown motel on Memorial Highway. This area was notorious for prostitution and crime. When we pulled up, there were a lot of shady characters around the entrance. My team positioned themselves around the building in unmarked cars to be inconspicuous to the locals. The tracker in Danelle's purse led us to room 210, and we positioned ourselves outside the room. We could overhear two women talking. One sounded stressed, and the other was aggressive. We wanted to move quickly to ensure Danelle's safety. Lavonna had Danielle tied to a chair while she walked around the room, yelling at her. Danielle appeared to be bruised up but still alive. As far as we could see, Lavonna wasn't holding a gun in her hands or nearby. She was so fixated on Danielle that she didn't even look up once to notice us crouched at the window. This was our perfect chance to disrupt the scene. I gave my men the count to ambush the perv. "On the count of 3, team", I whispered. "1.2.3." Bang! We burst in the door with guns in the air, catching Lavonna by surprise. "DeKalb County police department, Lavonna, you are under arrest for the kidnapping of Danielle Streeter and the Murder of Katrina Cook!"I yelled. "I am not armed; I am not armed!" Lavonna screamed. "Detective James, please read this young lady her rights and put her in handcuffs," I alerted my partner. "My pleasure," Detective James replied. "Danielle, are you alright?," I asked. "Yes, Detective Rodgers, thank you for saving my life," Danielle replied. "No. Thank you for keeping that tracker in your purse," I said. "We would never have located you if you didn't have it," I added. "I am just lucky she didn't throw my purse away like she did my phone," Danielle said. "Let's get to the ER to make sure you are OK," I said. I assisted Danielle down the stairs into my car. Detective James walked Lavonna to his vehicle in handcuffs to transport her back to the station.

On the ride to the hospital, we informed Danielle that Eric was out of the ICU and had been in recovery for the past few weeks. We expect him to go to rehab and then home. I explained that the nurses say that he has been recovering and will be back on his feet in no time. She asked if she could visit him once she got done in the ER. I told her yes. Since Lavonna was in custody, she told Danielle everything about the shooting and the murder. We learned we had the right culprit, and Eric was out of danger. Ms. Streeter was very lucky. The nurse alerted us she only had a few scratches and bruises, but otherwise, she would be OK. I escorted her to the private wing we had. Mr. Eric was recovering. I walked away and let them have a moment because I am sure they got a lot to discuss.

This was a crazy night that could've gone terribly, but I'm glad we got Lavonna in custody, and this nightmare is over. Meanwhile, at the station, Lavonna sat in the interrogation room quietly. Her face did not show any signs of remorse, and I recognized then that we were dealing with a person with the classic symptoms of a psychopath. Lavonna admitted to everything. We found out that she was in Atlanta for months before the shooting, but it made us assume she was in New York the whole time. If you did all this for custody of your daughter, you might as well kiss your child goodbye. She has to grow up without her mother because the charges we presently have against you come with some serious time. "I don't care. I just couldn't let him get custody of her. She's my daughter. I gave birth to her. She's mine!" she yelled. "She is also his daughter too," I added, " What you did was unspeakable, and I am glad you are behind bars." Lavonna was then quickly escorted down the hall to another room to get booked and fingerprinted. We walked her down another hall in silence and placed her in a jail cell to await her court hearing in the morning.

They say a love for a child is great, but did she really have to kill people because of it? I've seen people do crazy things in dysfunctional relationships, but this case took the cake. She doesn't really love anyone but herself. I picked up my cell to call to check up on Danielle to make sure she got home. She said after talking to Eric, Steve came to pick her up from the hospital. "Everything was crazy today, but I am glad Eric and I spoke," Danielle said. "I told him I hated that the shooter was his wife, and I could sympathize with him and how he will have to tell his daughter this horrible truth one day", she added. She wished him the best, and she was happy that he can get his daughter now. "Yeah, me too," I responded. I explained that the mother had too much emotional baggage to raise a little girl. I added that that little girl would've suffered from all the stuff Lavonna was dealing with. She was a psychopath and had no remorse for anything she did. "Detective, I noticed I was stuck in a dirty hotel with her all night," Danielle laughed. "Although Eric is a womanizer, I assume he's learned his lesson and is ready to take on his responsibility as a dad"; she added. "Yeah, from what I've heard tonight, I felt he was glad when I talked to him and facing near death", I explained. "This entire experience was enough to change his outlook on life and hopefully, he learns to take things more seriously and take people's emotions more seriously is it as well," Danielle said. "Yeah, those emotions are tricky, especially when you don't recognize what kind of mindset a person is in," I added. "That is the truth detective, " Danielle replied. "I'm just glad that I made it out alive, and I will continue to enjoy my life and leave it to the fullest," she added." If there's anything you need before the trial date, please call me. This is not over, but at least we caught the bad guy. I'm sorry that you had to get kidnapped tonight," I said jokingly. "At least I am still living to tell you about it, Detective Rodgers," Danielle joked back. "Yes, you are!" I exclaimed, "I will talk to you later, Ms. Streeter, and tell my buddy Steve hello." "I will do it," Danielle replied. "Thank you for everything, detective," she added and "Good night". She then hangs up the phone. Yeah, I guess Miss Danielle's going to be alright.

44. Danielle

"Steve drove us back to the house. I am so glad you are alright, baby," he said. "If anything had happened to you, I don't know what I would have done," he added. Tears well into his eyes as he whispered to me. "I love you so much, and you are my everything," Steve whispered. "You are mine," I whispered as I kissed him. "Tonight went well. I have to say", Steve spoke. "The person who shot you is behind bars, and besides that, you didn't get shot again," he said, laughing. "Ha ha ha, you're funny," I said, hitting him in the shoulder. "Things are gonna be a little different, Mr. Stevo, and a lot less scary," I said. "I am so glad that my life is returning to normal," I added. "You would never have to worry about any crazy chicks after me because you are the only woman in my life," Steve replied. We continued our drive to Steve's apartment, admiring the city lights. I started reminiscing about all the past few years' events since I moved to the city. I am totally grateful for having met such a kind and sexy man. Steve has brought so much joy to my life, even though the low points. I feel so blessed at this moment.

The next morning, after a crazy night, I woke up with breakfast in bed with a red rose in a vase. "What did I do to get such a perfect morning," I asked with a smile. Steve smiled back with a smile that lit up the entire room. "I have something to ask you, but I need you to lift the napkin on your tray first," Steve asked with a mischievous grin. There was a napkin that appeared to be covering something. It was a small box. I opened the box and inside was the most beautiful ring I had ever laid eyes on. "Is this what I think it is?" I asked Steve with tears in my eyes. "Yes, it is. Will you, Danielle Streeter, take me always and forever? Will you be my wife?" he asked. "Yes, baby, always and forever!" I screamed. We kissed each other as we had never before and made love all morning. I finally got the happy ending I deserved.

45. Eric

Lavonna had her trial today. They convicted her for 50 years for the murder of Trina, 20 for my attempted murder, and another 20 for the attempted murder and kidnapping of Danielle Streeter. They called the murder a crime of passion, so she didn't get the death penalty. She is likely to die in prison either way, but I think she should have gotten life. I finally could finish all the proceedings and paperwork for my little girl. After wrapping my arms around my little girl and feeling joy in my heart, I can't compare it. I am really sad that she will have to grow up without her mother. However, her mother is a dangerous woman. She was so selfish that she never once thought about how her actions could have affected her daughter. All she wanted to do was beat me, and she almost did. I almost lost my life because she was obsessed with winning. My daughter will move in with me this week, and I've already got her school situation workout. As for my love life, I have learned a lot from my near-death experience. I learned that you have to be careful with matters of the heart. Everyone deserves to be loved, but they also deserve honesty. I absolutely adored Danielle, but I was not honest with her, and I lost her because of my lies. I will never forgive myself for what I've done, but I have learned from my mistakes. I will never enter a relationship unless I'm done with everyone, and I can dedicate myself to

only that one person. No more playing games.
That life is over for me.

46 My Day (Danielle)

""Oh my God, mom, I am so nervous about today," I said. "What makes you so nervous, sweetheart? You've been dreaming about this since you were a little girl. You are so beautiful today," Mom said. "I just made so many mistakes in my relationships. I'm just hoping that this is the right one", I replied. "What is your heart telling you?" she said. "This guy has been there through all the drama and pain," she said. "He's a good man, Danielle, and he loves you dearly," she added. Mom, "I love him so much with every breath of my body," I exclaimed. "Well, what are you nervous about?" she said. "Get your butt up there and walk down that aisle now".

The wedding venue is on the beach in a beautiful location in the Bahamas. A small group of my closest family and friends are in attendance. My sisters, of course, were my bridesmaids, and I dressed them in a light pink front cowl neck and a V-back dress with spaghetti straps, and a pleated mermaid skirt with a sexy leg slit. My sisters were looking hot!

Who would've thought I would marry the man of my dreams today? As I was getting ready, my dad surprised me. "Oh my God, I can't believe you are here?" I said. "I wouldn't have missed this day for anything," he said. "I finally got to walk one of my girls down the aisle," he said.

On the way to the beach, I grabbed onto my dad's arm and walked down the ramp. One of my close friends is singing my favorite song, *I want you,* by Brian McKnight. As I walk down the path of roses on the sand, I see Steve standing with a big smile and tears running down his cheeks. I see all the people I love sitting on chairs on the beach. They all stand as I walk past them with my dad. I reach the altar and take hold of Steve's hand. I look into his eyes, and I know -at this moment - it's more than just me. It's now just us.

Made in the USA
Columbia, SC
19 February 2024

32004896R00095